"Now see what you've done."

"Me? What the devil have I done?" Sam demanded to know. "One little kiss..."

"*Little?*"

"So maybe medium sized. And for that I get a raucous lecture, a slap in the face and an accusation about me and my daughter that's right out of the clear blue sky. Just what made you think I was offering to make you my daughter's stepmother?"

Had he said a word about that? Or had she, in her usual haste, managed to put the cart before the horse again?

Sam Horton stepped closer. "Can't think of an answer?" he probed.

"No, I can't," Rose said defiantly. "But I'll keep trying...."

Dear Reader,

It's raining men! Welcome to Harlequin Romance's new miniseries, **Holding Out For A Hero**. Every month for a whole year we'll be bringing you some of the world's most eligible men. They're handsome, they're charming but, best of all, they're single! And as twelve lucky women are about to discover, it's not finding Mr. Right that's the problem—it's holding on to him!

We kick off the series with an all-American hero courtesy of ever-popular author Emma Goldrick. *Husband Material* (#3392) is the story of local widow Rose Mary Chase, who dreams of meeting the one man capable of sweeping her off her feet! A man like Sam Horton, in fact—now, there's a guy who would make a perfect husband. He already is a great dad to his young daughter, Penny. And Penny knows that all they need to make a perfect family is Rose!

In the coming months look out for books with our **Holding Out For A Hero** flash by some of Harlequin Romance's best-loved authors: Leigh Michaels, Jeanne Allan, Betty Neels, Lucy Gordon and Rebecca Winters. Next month it's the turn of Catherine George with *Fallen Hero*. This is one series you don't want to miss!

With best wishes,

The Editors
Harlequin Romance

Some men are worth waiting for!

Husband Material
Emma Goldrick

Harlequin Books

TORONTO • NEW YORK • LONDON
AMSTERDAM • PARIS • SYDNEY • HAMBURG
STOCKHOLM • ATHENS • TOKYO • MILAN
MADRID • WARSAW • BUDAPEST • AUCKLAND

This book is dedicated to our son, Robert, a
Licensed Private Detective, who always worries us
when we write about Breaking and Entering.

ISBN 0-373-03392-3

HUSBAND MATERIAL

First North American Publication 1996.

CHAPTER ONE

ROSE MARY CHASE was a small baby. When her uncle John carried her to the baptismal font in the Episcopal church in Padanaram, he could hold her in one hand. "Rose," he told the Bishop. "Rose Mary. A holy terror, but she'll grow." She had, of course, but not very much. And when Rose was twenty-seven she gave up her crusading ways and settled down. Uncle John and all her other relatives were dead by that time, including her husband, Frank Hamilton, and she had only Millie O'Doul to look after her.

Padanaram was an unusual village. Over the course of a century or more inhabitants had gone down to the sea in ships, and had been fruitfully rewarded. As the elders died off their fortunes passed down, usually to widows or single daughters. So eventually Padanaram contained a large cluster of widows or daughters who believed in the old adage never to spend your principle; to live off your interest and live frugally.

Rose Chase was one of these. Not the oldest, nor the richest, but still one of the "old money" inheritors. A widow, too. Her young husband, a Hamilton, had been killed in a hit-and-run auto accident almost a year past. Rose had set her red-headed mind to survival, and life went on.

On August fourteenth, at two in the afternoon, Rose was standing in her front yard, leaning on her swinging gate, daydreaming.

5

"Is this 16 Middle Street?" A deep voice. Bass, she told herself as she peeped out from under her straw bonnet. Deep bass.

A man; husky but not big, to be truthful, dressed in blue suit and tie, carrying a wicker basket over one massive arm, its contents covered with a light dishcloth. Rose, usually quick of tongue, gasped at him. She had met many men, but none so magnificent as this one. He took her breath away.

"16 Middle Street?" he asked. "Little girl?"

"Little girl"? One thing Rose hated was condescension. "Little girl" indeed! She glared up at him and took a deep breath. She was wearing an old summer dress; it could barely contain her. "I am not," she said coldly, "a *little* girl."

He chuckled. Massively. Deeply. "Yes, I can see that," he answered solemnly. "Is your mother home?"

"I'm afraid not."

"Perhaps your father? Your aunt?"

"For whom are you looking?" Rose crossed her fingers. She was a few years out of the University of Massachusetts, and had only a flighty memory of pronouns and verbs, possessive, recessive, or whatever. She ducked her head behind her bonnet; he didn't seem to mind.

"I'm looking for Mrs. Chase," he said. "One of my neighbors at the other end of the block recommended that I contact Mrs. Chase with my problem." He lifted his basket and rested it on top of the stone wall.

"Oh, you're selling something? We've already bought at the office."

"No, I'm not selling anything." She could feel the impatience in his voice. His size caused her to back off a step or two. "And who is this Mrs. Chase?"

Rose took a deep breath. "Me," she said. "I."

"You have to be kidding! You're a—"

"I am Mrs. Chase," she said firmly. "The only one in town. And just who might you be?" It was impossible to hold her breath any longer. She exhaled gustily and her bodice seemed to shrink an inch or two. Then she squared her shoulders.

He studied her warily, his bronze face turning just the slightest bit darker. "Horton," he said. "Sam Horton." She waited for something more, some definition, some listed occupation. But Sam remembered his instructions, up in the office of the attorney general in Boston. "We've had all kinds of investigators poke around down there, Horton, and he evaded them all. You've got to keep undercover. Say that you're a—oh, I don't know— a book salesman. You could open a bookstore and—"

But opening a bookstore in a village as tiny as Padanaram was no easy thing. "Bookstore, hell," he had muttered on his way out to his car. "I'll make believe I'm a lawyer, which I am."

Who would believe that? Not even the parking-meter lady.

"Even was you the governor's brother," she had said as she'd written the ticket.

"That wasn't too smart." His twelve-year-old daughter had been curled up in the back seat of the car, watching as he tore the ticket up. He'd growled at her; he hated young female critics, even his own.

So here in Padanaram he clamped his mouth shut in front of this lovely girl and shoved his basket over in front of her as a ploy. "I'm opening a law office," he said. "Well, in fact I'm scouting around town for a suitable location."

Rose shook her head. A law office in one of the smallest villages in Massachusetts? The man had rocks in his head! But then she wasn't here to censor, and the cover on the basket wiggled interestingly.

"I know just the man for you to see," she said warily. "Chad Westbrook, my broker. Out of an old Yankee family." Which, as any resident of Padanaram would know, guaranteed his quality. But this beautiful Mr. Horton didn't seem to recognize the code.

He gave her a curious look, acting as if he was waiting for her to say something else. Instead the light cloth cover quivered—wiggled, actually—and pulled free at one corner. And a gunmetal-gray kitten pushed her nose out into the sunshine and mewed. A tiny thing with the tiniest stub of a tail; hardly no tail at all.

"A kitten!" Rose exclaimed. "You're selling kittens!" The joy faded. "But we don't need a kitten—I don't think. How much are you charging?"

Trapped, Sam Horton thought quickly. "Not selling," he commented. "Giving. You like kittens?"

"Love them."

The kitten was nursing on Rosie's little finger. And then, as she watched, entranced, the cover wiggled again.

"Twice as much love, then," he said. "Two for the price of one. No charge. And the basket thrown in for a quick bargain."

The other little feline managed to get his head out. "Twins?" Rose reflected, enchanted.

"Twins," he affirmed. "Weaned and inoculated."

The first kitten was still gnawing on Rosie's finger. The second moved over to join in the nourishment. Little kittens had sharp fangs. She moved her finger gingerly out of the way.

"Let me show you," he said as he pulled the second little animal out and held it in one hand. The little stub of its tail wiggled enthusiastically. The hot summer sun broke through its clouds and the little cat's gray fur sparkled.

"Lovely," Rose murmured, all her innate love of the young rushing out through her eyes. "But—come in the house. Millie has to see." She tugged at his massive arm. "I have to ask her. We share the house, you know."

"Ask me what?" Millie asked from the front door.

"Ask you if you could resist such adorable kittens," the man said.

"Before we take anything," Millie said, "we like to know who is giving it away. And why."

"Oh," he said as he ran his hand through his short hair. "I'm Sam Horton. My daughter and I just moved here from Boston and her cat, Beatrice, just had these two kittens. I'm a—er—looking to open a law office here in the village."

"A lawyer?" Millie sounded as if the fish she had bought for supper had just gone bad. "I don't think there'll be much business for you here in Padanaram."

"Don't make the man stand out here in the sun," Rosie interjected. "Come on in, Sam, and bring the kittens." As she opened the front door she turned and asked again, "You say they've been weaned?"

Following Millie into the house, he said, "Yes, ma'am. They're four months old today. They've both been weaned."

"How does your daughter feel about giving away her kittens?" Rosie asked from the back of the line.

"My daughter is resigned," Sam said as they entered the kitchen. He crossed his fingers behind his back. "I'm allergic to cats. The only reason my daughter gets to keep Beatrice is that she's had the cat for nearly all her life."

"Come sit down," Millie invited him. "Have a cold drink."

"No, thanks," he demurred; "I've got to get back. Penelope gets upset if I'm away too long."

"How old is she?" Millie asked.

"Penny is twelve, going on thirteen," he said. "Do we have a deal? Will you take one of the kittens?"

Millie picked one of the animals up and after looking said, "What happened to their tails? These kittens don't have tails."

"Sorry," Sam drawled, "I only give them away; I don't explain genetic shortfalls."

"Well, thank you, Mr Horton," Rosie said quickly before Millie could uncover his life history. "Yes, we'll take them both. Let me show you out."

Millie looked affronted, but Sam stood up, and seemed to fill the small kitchen. "I'm sure you'll get a barrel of enjoyment from the kittens. What do you suppose you'll name them?" He knew where the power of the household lay. He spoke to Millie, who was now holding both of the squirming little felines.

"Too Soon," Millie said, taking precautionary measures to keep her tongue from wagging out of synch. "And the other one probably Too Late. The Too twins."

He masked a grin and shook his head at her. "Too much," he said softly, and made for the door, following Rosie's trim figure.

Going from the bright kitchen where Rosie had installed extra windows, they plunged into the semi-darkness of the front room. Sam was blinded for the moment it took his eyes to adjust. He didn't see that Rosie had stopped. He ran into her and, having her in his arms, he decided to do what he'd wanted to do since he'd first seen her. He bent down and kissed her. She was so taken aback that she let it happen. It felt so nice that she contributed to the whole experiment. Just for a second, of course. And then she broke away.

"Well, really! Aren't you a married man?"

"I was but she divorced me a few years ago," he said. "You know, I'm going to like living here in Padanaram." He moved to the door and opened it. "Surely you're not married?"

"Widow," Rose said through clenched teeth. "My husband was murdered some years ago."

Oh, boy, he told himself. Widow? Murdered? Luckily for him, he went out the door and walked down the path to the sidewalk before Rose could gather her senses.

"A lot of man," Millie said after a moment from her place at the kitchen door. "Good-looking."

"Oh? I thought he was—homely. Big, though. Big and homely?"

"You're seeing with your druthers," Millie said. "You'd druther he wasn't too good-looking, because then your radio station would have to be nice to him."

"Me? Be nice to a—lawyer? And didn't he sound so tentative about that? I'll wager a nickel to a doughnut he hasn't won a single case so far this year. Lawyer? Hah!"

Rose turned her back on her housekeeper and delved into the kitten basket. The pair of them came to her hand and twined themselves around her wrist.

"The kittens are handsome," she commented. "And the basket is out of this world! What a nice addition to the neighborhood."

"Him?"

"No. Them." She plunged her hand back into the kitten basket.

Radio Station WXBN blared in her ear. Rock and roll for a Sunday afternoon. "Turn that darned radio down. Who ever convinced me that we needed hard rock on a Sunday afternoon?"

"It's your station and your music," Millie said. "If you don't like it you can cancel. And fire the program director. Besides, I like it!"

"And if I canceled," Rose said glumly, "we'd lose all of our Sunday afternoon kiddie audience."

"And it's the kids who spend the money," Millie commented.

"I like it," Millie repeated. "Take a note, kid. He's good-looking, employed and single."

"What are you trying to do to me?" Rose complained wearily. "Every time there's a new man in the neighborhood you keep pushing me at him. Most of them don't become interested until they hear about my money. I'm a career woman, not a prospective housewife. I operate a two-hundred-and-fifty-watt commercial radio station."

"I've got light bulbs that big in my closet," Millie snapped. "You're not married. That's the important thing in a girl's life. Seems a shame."

"I'm single by choice. I've *been* married. It's not all that it's cracked up to be. And besides, he's encumbered."

"He's what?"

"Encumbered. With a daughter. You heard him. Why would any sensible woman rush to become the wicked stepmother?" There was only one way to win an argument with Millie. Rose took it. The screen door slammed behind her before her housekeeper could muster an answer, but even as far as the fence Rose could hear her muttering.

The sun was really hot. Sam Horton stopped at the corner of Franklin Street and fished out a handkerchief. Crazy, he told himself. I know housing's in short supply, but I never expected to wind up in a neighborhood like this. Mrs. Moltry is a society maven and expects me to join her set. The lady next to her reads palms and does astrology charts. The next house is empty. And then we have Mrs. Chase and company. Lord knows what her specific problem is; witchcraft, maybe? She lives in a madhouse.

But she's cute, his conscience demanded. He shrugged. The attorney general back in Boston had assured him this was only a *temporary* assignment. And it's true, he thought. She is cute!

His house was not as large as Rose Chase's, which had two floors and at least twelve rooms and a swimming pool out back. But his had plenty of land around it, now set in tired sawgrass and weeds. A little imagination could make a garden, or even a swimming pool for Penelope. He looked around for his daughter. She loved to be out in the sun.

Penny was at the side of the house, sitting stiffly upright in her wheelchair, her nurse hovering at attention nearby. There hadn't been much sunlight at their Boston apartment. The child looked like a pale ghost. Long blond hair, hanging straight as a die down her back; pale cheeks, except for the red splotch—red splotch?— just beside her mouth. Gray-green eyes. Massive eyes for a girl just turning thirteen. A dress hid the upper steel structure of the braces that provided support which her muscles could not furnish. A red splotch adorned her left cheek...

Red splotch? As if someone— "Mrs. Harrold?"

"Good morning, Mr. Horton."

"Good morning, Mrs. Harrold. How has Penelope been so far today?"

The woman was built like a block of granite, with a face that hadn't smiled since Caesar crossed the Rubicon. "Naughty," she grumbled. "All day long. Whining and complaining about everything. And she wouldn't eat her breakfast. I was forced to punish her."

He looked down at his daughter. Her chin was stuck out as if she was determined to outface the world. Lord, what am I into? he asked himself. I haven't the slightest idea how to raise a girl-child!

The girl rolled one of the wheels of her chair to turn her more toward him. As she did so the bright sun outlined her figure in what was an extremely thin dress. The words he had planned to speak stuck in his craw. I can't manage her in her childhood, he snarled at himself, and while I'm trying to learn how, she's growing older by the minute! Why me, God?

He leaned over and took one of her thin, almost wasted hands in his own and squeezed gently. Four years since his divorce, two years since he had taken over the care and direction of this child of his. Holding the gentle hand, he looked over at Mrs. Harrold.

"You mean you hit her?"

"That's what you have to do with children who don't behave," the nurse reported grimly. "Take the strap to her. That's what the Bible says."

"Does it really?" he commented in a voice as mild as Ivory soap. He reached into his pants pocket.

"Yes. Raise them in the Fear of the Lord," the nurse continued in a very self-satisfied tone.

"I don't exactly think that's what the Bible meant," Sam Horton said. "Especially in regard to a girl who's been confined to a wheelchair for most of her natural life."

"God's punishment," Mrs. Harrold commented. "Brought it on herself, I expect."

Sam gritted his teeth. "It's hard to be a father," he returned. "It takes a great deal of patience." He pulled his hand out of his pocket and counted a couple of bills off a money-roll big enough to choke a horse. He pushed them into the nurse's hands and folded her fingers over them.

"I don't think you and I are ever going to get along. I would appreciate it if you would move out of here today. This noontime, to be exact."

"Well, I never!"

"Certainly never again," he said. "Do yourself a favor, Mrs. Harrold. Don't ever appear in my house again for any purpose. I don't think I could be as full of the milk of human kindness as I ought!"

The nurse tilted her head high in the air, sniffed at the pair of them, and made for the gate at high speed. Father and daughter watched as the woman climbed into her car parked at the curb and zoomed off.

Sam Horton bent over and scooped his daughter out of the wheelchair. "So there," he chuckled.

"But you shouldn't have," the girl said solemnly. "We've been in town here for four days and you've already fired two nurses. It didn't hurt."

"The firing didn't hurt?"

"No, silly. The hitting. She's not very strong. I enjoyed the firing."

He cuddled her close to his massive chest. "There'll be no hitting in my family," he said. "None!"

"But Mama hit me all the time."

"And that's why we were divorced, love."

"If I was a cute little tyke she wouldn't have, Daddy."

"You *are* a cute little tyke," he exhorted. "Cute as a button."

"That's all right for you and me to say, but how come there's no other woman in the world who agrees with you?"

"There's bound to be somebody else," he insisted as he swung her up in his arms and started for the door. "Somewhere in this wide, wide world there's a nice woman who thinks just the way I do—about you, that is." He held his daughter at the door, and waited for the child to turn the doorknob. Somewhere there has to be, he told himself grimly. And I've got to find her. I don't care how many rotten traits she has, just so long as she loves Penelope Horton!

"I tried, Pa. I tried to be nice to both of them, but I was scared. I didn't—"

"I don't blame you, love. They were both too old. Are you hungry?"

"Mmm."

"Come on, there's still some of that crunchy peanut butter left."

"Another peanut butter sandwich? One of us has got to learn how to cook before we both starve to death."

"I agree, baby. You?"

"Not me. I'm too young."

"And I'm too old."

"I know a heck of a good way to get some nice woman to take care of us," Penelope Horton said. "Why don't you get married again?"

He shook his head slowly. "I don't know, love. I tried that once. It didn't work."

"That's because you didn't do it right. My mother couldn't boil water without burning it. Now, if we really put our minds to it we could look around and find someone who can cook and bake and sew, and like that, and—"

"*We* could?"

"*We* could. This is too important to be left just to some dumb man! I know just what *we* want."

"And of course *I* don't?"

"You surely don't," the child said. "We might even find one that's sort of—well—sexy. You'd like that."

Sam Horton looked down at his daughter. She looked up at him. Twelve years old was too early by far for all this. Carefully he lowered her into her indoor chair, moved her gently over to the window, and raised the shade to let the light in. She was wearing a shoestring sundress. It might have been green at one time; now it was nondescript. It was too tight at the top and too short

at the bottom, and even a blind man could have seen
that his little girl was well over the threshold of puberty.

Oh, my lord, he muttered to himself. I haven't even
learned how to handle her in her formative years. Why
is it all happening to me—and all at once?

His daughter, who had outstanding hearing for a girl
of her age, also had the brain to dissemble. "It's that
red wallpaper on the walls." she said. "It makes everything appear dull. We hafta get things straight around
this crazy place."

At the other end of the row of houses Rose Chase, still
mooning in her front yard, heard the crash of thunder
and looked up. A massively black cloud came racing in
from the southwest, spurred on by a breeze that
strengthened by the moment. It was threat enough.

She looked around her tiny front yard, where the grass
was brown and sere instead of waving green. August was
always this way. Short on green and water, long on sun
and beaches and swimming. New England had four full
seasons, and one had better develop a love for them all,
or move.

But she had delayed too long. A very large raindrop
splatted across her nose, as if the Wampanoag Rain God
was laughing at her. She plucked up her skirts and ran
for the house.

Millie was waiting there, holding the screen door open.
"Left it a little late, didn't we?"

The words were unnecessary. In just those eight or
nine running steps it took for her to reach the tiny porch
the clouds had opened on her, and she was so soaked
that her dress clung.

"You look like a drowned mouse," her housekeeper
told her. "Another five minutes and I would've called
the rescue squad. Here. Take this." Millie had come prepared, with a massive bath towel in her hand. She threw

it in Rose's direction. With the background of much
practice Rose caught the towel and dropped it over her
head.

"Rub it in," Millie commanded, and then immediately moved to do the rubbing for herself. Rose chuckled.
It always came to this. Millie would never admit that
her little Rose had grown up, that she could think and
move and do for herself.

"Don't know enough to come in out of the rain," the
old lady muttered through gritted teeth as she rubbed to
the best of her strength. "I don't know how you keep
that radio station afloat." Which was a line she always
used, a line Rose had learned to put up with without a
sarcastic come-back.

"Now hop upstairs and change into something dry.
Lord, what's the world coming to these days?"

"Armageddon?" Rose offered as she dashed for the
stairs. She almost stumbled over the railed transport chair
they had needed to help Frank up the stairs.

"And don't be smart," Millie called after her. "You're
still not too old to get a good paddling!"

Rose knew better. Her last paddling had come about
when she was two years old, when she had, with malice
aforethought, bitten her father's hand. And learned the
axiom about the hand that fed you.

Thereafter she had quickly discovered that honey
turned more blows than vinegar. She stripped as she
went, dropping her dress here, her bra there, her shoes
wherever. "And dry yourself off before you put on
something different," Millie yelled from downstairs.
With a smile on her little round face Rose complied, and
found herself confronting the massive mirror hanging
on the wall of the bathroom, nude.

It was the one attitude that always surprised her. Normally she paid little or no attention to her appearance.
She brushed her curly red hair regularly—one hundred

strokes daily—covered herself daily with some dress of some color, and let it go at that. Usually it was a dress that Millie had bought for her because her "baby" just didn't have the time or skill for shopping. Her baby, twenty-seven years old. From time to time Rose rebelled, but mostly she enjoyed the pampering, and only occasionally found herself confronting herself. As now.

There was no doubt about it. Her breasts were too big. Without more care they would begin to sag. Not yet, but some day soon. She cupped them with both hands. They were still firm, thank the Lord. Nothing she hated worse than the thought of sagging. She turned to one side in front of the mirror. There was a comfortable little balloon around her hips as well. That needed to come off PDQ—Pretty Darn Quick.

And her hair... Lord, what a mess. A russet forest of curls, her mother used to say. But with a jaundiced eye it was a rage of red. She leaned over to pick up her hairbrush. Nothing sagged. That was a relief. She attacked the jungle on top of her head.

Millie came upstairs just as she finished dressing. "Ham for supper? Canned. Potatoes? What else?"

"Spinach?" Rose was busy trying to braid her short hair into two plaits, with little success.

"I don't know why you do that," Millie said, staying the brush momentarily. "It only stays in place for—"

"For an hour," Rose interjected. "Maybe even more on a rainy day. But at least for an hour I can look neat."

"You planning to go out on a date tonight?"

Rose turned away from the mirror, surprised. "Now where in the world would *I* go on a Sunday night, and with whom?"

Millie gestured at Rose's bedroom. "You ask me? Who in the world would live in a pure white bedroom at your age? Virginal Manor? You've been a widow for—"

"Twelve months," Rose supplied.

"Twelve months. And you're still living in the room that you've used since you were five years old. Why aren't you up and around? Why don't you redecorate the master bedroom and move back there again? *Why* are you home with not a date in sight on a Sunday night?"

"Oh, come on, Millie. You know all the answers. You tell me."

"I don't know this answer. Don't tell me that you're still wearing the willow for your husband?"

"And why not?"

"You know why not. You were darn near to divorcing him before that—that man ran him down."

Rose whirled around to face her housekeeper. Her face turned pale. She almost looked a perfect match for her white-painted walls. "Don't you say that, Millie," she said fiercely. "Don't you ever say that again!"

"Why not? It's true."

"It may be true, but—he was a hard man to live with, what with all his medical problems. And when he was killed I felt so—guilt-ridden, Millie!" Her normal contralto rose to a panicky pitch. "It doesn't matter—all those little arguments between Frank and me. So he wasn't a perfect husband, but he was a volunteer hero for the United Nations in Somalia, and he came home and died a hero!"

Rose was still pale as a sheet, not red-faced. She steadied herself, forced her feelings back down her throat, and stabbed at her left eye with her knuckle. It was the eye that always had the tendency to leak.

She needed something to take her mind off the subject. She picked up the brush and started on her hair again.

Millie shrugged and, forced by long habit, went back out into the hall, to the trail of clothing that Rose had left while undressing, and began to pick up the discarded material. Rose let one plait escape her before she

sealed it with an elastic. It fell down and immediately
returned to its curly nature. She shrugged into her robe
and sat down on the edge of her bed and started again.

What if... ? Her mind buzzed. What if I had a date
with Sam Horton? Lawyer Sam?

Both her mother and father would have been proud
of her, walking out with a lawyer. A businessman above
the usual trade, entitled to call himself "Esquire".
Although somehow or another he didn't seem to quite
fill the bill. And besides, both her parents were gone.

And what if she and the lawyer made a thing out of
it? Certainly he would have a great deal of influence in
the village—after a time, that was. Yankee villages tended
to move very slowly. Maybe even enough influence to
force the district attorney into discovering and bringing
her husband's murderer to trial on some charge. Murder?
How could it have happened? Struck down in the middle
of Middle Street. Run down by a hit-and-run driver, in
the darkness of a rainy night and not a single witness to
be found.

What if... ? What if Sam Horton turned out to be a
secret FBI agent, with a lot of power?

What if he kissed me again? she wondered. Oh, wow!
There was nothing small-time about his kissing. Nothing
bad at all. Just imagine we were married and had three
children of our own and lived in a big house across the
bay, up on the hill near Colonel Green's former estate,
and every single night we—!

And down at the other end of the block Sam Horton
stood with spatula in hand over the gas stove, trying to
construct a couple of hamburgers. But his mind wasn't
really on his work. He could see Rose Chase standing
in *his* kitchen, dressed in practically nothing. No, that
wouldn't do. His kitchen walls were a dingy depository
for more frying grease than his skillet could hold. The

kitchen would have to be redone before he could get Rose into it. But how about upstairs?

In the master bedroom. That had been redecorated just before he'd bought the house. And the bed was massive. Rose Chase, delightfully dressed in moonbeams. He would lead her to the bed and she would fall back down on the mattress and smile at him, and they would—if only Penelope didn't interrupt!

But then Penny, with her wheelchair, lived on the ground floor, while the other bedrooms were upstairs!

"What in the world are you doing, Dad?" Penelope. Astonished, he was back in the kitchen staring at the spiral of smoke rising from the blackened hamburgers. Was it a bad thing to swear at your daughter? he asked himself. Probably. Even if you didn't say it aloud?

Shaking his head in disgust, Sam Horton set the spatula down on the top of the stove and turned off the gas before he moved to hug his daughter. Hugging was not a thing he had done much of in past years. Too busy? His conscience had begun to bother him some time during the last four weeks. "I've not been much of a father, have I?" he asked. Penelope did a double-take but did not respond. Maybe she was thinking the same thing?

"What do you say, Penny, if we go down to McDonald's for our supper?"

"Are you sure you're feeling all right?"

Your daughter is still mad at the world and all its people, he told himself. So we'll go anyway. Maybe we could stop by the Chase house and see if Rose would go with us? He shrugged. He knew it wouldn't work. Too completely different women, both angry with him at the same time. What a dinner party *that* would make! But—

But I'm not ready yet, he told himself. How about that? An outstanding record in law school. Editor of the *Harvard Law Review*. And on my first case I prosecute a man who commits murder and he walks away! And that's the end of my job with the district attorney. So the next thing I do when I move to a new town is to meet a woman whose husband has been murdered, and his murderer, she tells me, walks away too! Well, I'll do better. Damned if I don't!

CHAPTER TWO

MONDAY morning. Even the boss had to get up and go to work on Monday. Rose groaned and rolled over, ducking her head under the sheet. Not just a plain sheet. It was edged in lace, and embroidered with gamboling black or white lambs. Her grandmother's contribution from long years past. It matched the white-painted room. And the narrow iron bed, fit for a nun's repose.

"Rosie!" The shout from downstairs. The third shout of the day. Wearily Rose moved one foot out from under the sheet. Feet stomped up the stairs. "Rose Chase! You're five minutes late already. Is this the way to run a business?"

"No," she muttered, and shrugged the sheet tighter around her. No, the way to run a business is to neglect it, she thought. Let the employees run it. That's what they get paid for. I never wanted to be in the radio business—not ever. Or the boat business. Or the in-vestments-in-the-railroad business.

A heavy hand landed on her shoulders and gave a shake. "Makes a body think you don't *want* to own a radio station. Come on, Rose. We'd starve to death without WXBN."

I doubt that, Rose told herself. Since Great-Aunt Hattie had died the Chase bankroll had amounted to an eight-figure investment trust account, and a six-figure cash account. Once a year her three brokers forwarded a summary statement, which Rose hardly understood. Nevertheless, a penny saved was a penny earned—that was the family belief. So Rose made a supreme effort,

24

threw off the sheet, and rolled out onto the floor feet first. "I'm up; I'm up already."

"Looks like you spent the night waltzing with a mangy black bear," Millie announced as she held out a pink robe that didn't quite match Rosie's nightgown. "And I wish you'd *wear* that nightgown instead of just hanging it over the chair."

"What for?" Rose grumbled as she slipped into the robe. "I only keep it there in case we have a fire."

"Somebody might see you."

"Somebody did. I was six months married and never needed a nightgown."

"Rosie!"

"Well, it's true. Frank wanted a child right away. Do I shock you? What did you think we were doing behind that closed door? What's for breakfast?" Staccato conversation, fired at a round a second.

Millie flinched, but went on with her inquisition. "Hot oatmeal. Gives you strength. Orange juice. And I wish you wouldn't be so explicit in your conversations."

"That wasn't explicit, and I don't like oatmeal. Toast and coffee, and I'll be down in ten minutes."

"But—"

"Millie!"

"Black bear is right," the housekeeper muttered as she started back down the stairs. "Monday morning bad temper!"

Rose stretched like a cat, and headed for the bathroom. Black bear indeed. The bathroom was 1920s style, with the shower head located above the tub. Her father had meant to refurbish it years and years ago, only to find out that a new tub was too big to be taken up the stairs. So the old one still stood, with slightly chipped enamel, supported on four claw feet.

She climbed under the hot shower. Strange how little things upset her orderly life, she thought. The black bear is for real; his name is Sam Horton. And he lives just down the block. Damn the man, intruding on my very private dreams.

She dried herself off, brushed hair and teeth, and went back into her bedroom. Ordinarily she would have dressed with her door open. But for today, and for no good reason she could think of, she closed it behind her. Or maybe she did know why. Those dreams had been as explicit as the devil's brew! Things she thought she had forgotten. Things that Frank had taught her. Poor Frank. Out in the evening darkness on a trip to the grocery store, and run down not three or four houses from the house. Long gone. And Rose had never driven a car since.

"And so much for you, Sam Horton," she said as she plucked a navy blue suit from her closet and prepared to transfer herself from kitten-lover to maniac manager.

Kittens! With a flash of pleasure Rose remembered and dashed for the stairs. The rug on the fourth stair down was still worn, and once again she caught her toe in it and barely saved herself from a nosedive by grabbing madly at the seat of the little elevator. Despite its long disuse it started immediately and delivered her to the foot of the stairs in solemn dignity.

"The kittens," she yelled at Millie as she burst into the bright yellow kitchen.

"They were doing well until you yelled," Millie grumbled. "Now the pair of them are hiding under the table. And may I remind you that today's Monday, and somebody has to do something about these animals while I go grocery shopping?"

"You could put it off." Too excited to sit down, Rose stood at the table and gnawed on a piece of toast. "Put it off until Friday."

"When the kittens will be five days older, still not house-trained, and still require someone to watch them?"

"So we'll hire a sitter."

"A kitten-sitter?"

"What else? Surely there must be someone who—?"

"At this hour of a Monday morning? Not a chance. Sit down and eat your breakfast."

"So I'll take them to work with me!"

"That'll make a big hit," Millie grumbled. But not loudly enough to change Rose's mind.

And so Rose did. One in each of her deep jacket pockets, with their heads stuck out into the real world. And a container of milk added to her own brown paper bag lunch. Small local radio stations didn't make all *that* much money, especially when there were three much larger stations nearby in the city.

Millie escorted her to the door. "So you'll walk every day in spite of the fact that you own two cars?"

"Don't nag me, Millie. I'll walk every day providing it doesn't snow."

Millie made clucking noises as she watched her protégé go out into the hot August sun. "If it snows?" She clucked again, and then stopped. It *had* snowed in August once, in New England—1814, was it? The "year without a summer"? That was the year of the volcanic explosions around the rim of the world, and the snow had come on the fourth of July!

Rose sauntered down the hill toward town, counting the houses as she went. The entire harbor was on view, filled with yachts and splatters of sunshine. The sidewalk was uneven, with patched and repatched macadam or concrete slabs. In front of the first house, where Middle Street came to a dead end at Franklyn—*his* house—her pace faltered. There was nothing unusual about the place, except that *he* lived there. Somewhat on the order of snow in August, she told herself. You had to have the volcanoes before the snow came!

There was a girl sitting in a wheelchair by his gate. A child of indeterminate age. Not exactly a cute child, but smiling for all that. Her emaciated legs were fastened into steel braces. She was swinging the gate back and forth, using the electric motor on the wheelchair as a power source. It was more than the gate could stand. It squeaked and scraped.

The child gleefully ran her chair out onto the sidewalk as Rose approached. Rose made a quick assessment. The girl was already as big as Rose was, a little wider in a children's proportion, but obviously skating past the edge of puberty. Her hair could use a good brushing; her dress looked as if she had been outfitted from Good Will Industries.

"Lady?"

Rose stopped. The "child" really was as big as she was! Not unusual, of course. Most everything and everybody in Padanaram was as big as Rose Chase. Bigger, for that matter!

"Yes?"

"Would you like to buy a ticket for the Mothers Against Drunk Driving benefit ball?"

"Yes, I suppose so." Rose chuckled. She was vice president of MADD, and didn't need a ticket. But good salespeople had to be encouraged.

"The tickets are pricey," the child said with a calculating look. "You buying for just you or do you have a husband?"

"I'll be buying for just me," Rose said. "How much are they?"

"Twenty-five dollars a pop."

"Listen," Rose said, thinking that she was really running late, "I don't have that kind of money on me now but—" and she paused to think "—if you come down to the radio station later today, I can pay you then."

"Oh, wow! The radio station?" The girl did a couple of maneuvers around Rose. "You work there?" She was pretty clever with that chair, Rose thought. Lots of experience?

"Not exactly. I own it."

The child's eyes bugged out. "Wow! If you can cook too, you'll do."

"I'll do?" Rose checked her wristwatch and found that she was already fifteen minutes late, so a little more time hardly mattered. "Yes, I *can* cook, but I don't."

"You don't?"

"No. I hire a housekeeper. She cooks. And very nicely too."

"Jeez—!" The exclamation was quickly swallowed, to be replaced by, "Wow!"

"Yes, 'wow' is the correct word. And what's your name?"

"Penelope. They call me Penny. Are you under thirty?"

"I guess I could qualify for that—just barely."

"Well, that's not important. You look so nice that—oh, sh—sugar, that's a wedding ring on your finger? And you were only buying one ticket. I'm sorry; you won't do." She said it in a dull, dismal voice, as if her jar of joy had cracked and all the goodies had run out.

Rose held her left hand up into the sun. The diamond in her engagement ring was tiny, but it sparkled. The gold wedding band was turning green. Frank had not been a particularly good provider, but had refused to live off her money.

"I'm sorry about that—whatever it was you wanted me to do. I'm a widow. My husband—died." Listen to me, Rose told herself. I sound like a broken record. Frank's been dead—was murdered—months ago. Why can't I let him go?

"I really have to go. To work, you know. At the radio station." Rose offered another smile. The kittens in her pockets were restless. It had suddenly come to Rose's mind that two non-house-broken cats might just as well be non-pocket-broken cats as well, and that could be a disaster. So she waved a hand to the child, stepped over the huge sidewalk crack in front of the house, and continued on her way downtown.

Penny Horton watched her go, assessing her as she went. A little small, perhaps, but otherwise perfect. She can cook; she *has* a cook. She lives on our block. And she has a job at the radio station that plays all that wicked music! Wow. Wearing her first smile in a week, Penny turned her chair back toward the house. "Daddy," she yelled. "Daddy? Time to get up! Even self-employed lawyers have to work sometimes."

Sam Horton was not too pleased with the world. He came down still dressed in his yellow and red pajamas, hair all mussed, unshaven. His daughter moved away from the stairs. He had been to one of those typical "professional men's" parties the night before, where the liquor flowed like water. No telling how big a head he had! He was a wonderful father, but a girl never knew. At least, the kids in her school thought that way!

The kitchen table was set for two. Two knives, two forks, two bowls steaming with oatmeal. Add them on top of the wild dreams he had been having, and the day was already spoiled. He hated oatmeal. "Lawyers," he mumbled. "Don't ever let that detective business out. You hear?" He grumbled over to the table.

"Oatmeal. Yuck!" He picked up his bowl, carried it to the garbage disposal, and dumped its contents.

"That's not nice," his daughter complained angrily.

"Neither is oatmeal."

"That's all I know how to cook."

"It's a case of nothing being better than something. Don't we have any dry cereal?"

"Cornflakes," she returned bitterly. "Plain cornflakes." Penny hated cornflakes, unless they were the frosted kind. Her father was off on a save-the-teeth binge. Her teeth, that was. His own were almost perfect, and needed little saving.

He sat down at the table and brushed his hair back with both hands. His daughter drove to the counter and produced a battered box of flakes. "I'll take it," her father grumbled. She shrugged her bony shoulders and sighed. There was only one bowl left in the closet and practically no other dishes. The sink was full to bursting with dirty dishes.

Penny looked around angrily. If she mentioned dirty dishes her father would order her to wash them. Washing dishes was not her thing. She shrugged, took down the one clean bowl, and set it in front of him, along with the box of flakes and a spoon.

"Milk. We don't have any milk?"

"You know they don't deliver milk any more. Somebody has to go to the supermarket. We don't got no TV dinners, either."

"Don't have," her father corrected her. "No milk?"

"No milk."

"Then I might as well get dressed and go over to the diner."

"Yeah, that's great for you, but how about me?"

"You'll just have to come with me for breakfast. After that, I'll make up a list and call it in at that supermarket that delivers. Only no frosted flakes! I'll leave you some money to pay the delivery boy."

Penny's eyes lit up. She ducked her head so he could not see. All kinds of piracy were possible, and there were a dozen or more sugared flakes that were not called "frosted".

"Yeah, that would do it." She wiggled in her chair. "Daddy, I met this lady on the sidewalk this morning. She lives at the other end of the block."

"Ah? Speak up." He had resurrected his electric wet/dry shaver and was running the blade up and down the side of his face. The buzz was relatively quiet, but right under his ears.

Penny turned up her voice. She had had a great deal of experience lately in doing just that. "She has a cook. Would you believe that? A real live cook. Nice-looking lady, too."

"The cook? I think I met her yesterday."

"Not the cook, the lady."

Sam Horton snapped the switch on his razor and contemplated the jungle scene in his backyard before he turned back to his daughter. Yeah. Nice-looking lady. Just the type he'd like to take a tumble in bed with. Lord, she had more curves than a mountain railroad. "So what about this nice lady?"

"She was very pleasant to me. In fact, she bought a ticket to the MADD dohickey thing. We talked for a while. Did you know she's a widow?"

"Yes, I knew."

"She's gonna need a date to go to the thing," Penny continued artfully. "Why don't you take her to this ball? That way you could get to know her. You can see how 'sperienced she is. You wouldn't have to teach her everything, like you did with Mama."

"Ha!" he snorted, and then mumbled under his breath, "I never, ever had to teach your mother anything. She knew it all from the cradle." And then, louder, he said, "So what's the point, Penny?"

But his daughter, who was cleverer than the average bear, abandoned the subject entirely. "I'm going downtown today," the child said. "The lady said she'd have the money for the ticket at the radio station and

WXBN is offering free tours through the studio, and that scrumptious disc jockey is going to be there and..."

The words 'disc jockey' were the automatic cutout signal. While his daughter was still chattering on, the lawyer/detective's legal brain was already deep in the coils of the case that had brought him to the village. An intriguing little bit about an unknown investment counselor and embezzlement on a grand scale. Three more months—providing, of course, that the hare didn't run—and he'd have all the paperwork ready to send off to the federal prosecutors. And, since it was his father's bank that was being hit, the old guy might work up some better feelings for his son.

"Move things along," the district attorney had told him before he'd come down from Boston. "There are too many lawyers and bankers getting away with too many quiet little schemes. Get the information quickly; don't waste any time! Justice delayed is justice denied." That was a cliché which suited Sam Horton to a T. He turned his razor back on and finished shaving. And then the telephone rang.

His daughter raced for it. Since neither of them knew enough people in town to develop a following, ninety percent of their incoming calls were advertisements and fund-beggars, and Sam Horton had given up any attempt to answer for himself.

"It's for you. Boston." Her disgust was enough to fray the wires. He reached over and took the instrument from her and listened. Quietly at first, and then with some anger. His primary witness had been seen at Logan airport, boarding a plane for Trinidad! One more skip!

His daughter moved to the other side of the breakfast table for safety's sake. Obviously he was mad. Just as obviously he had forgotten what she had asked. "So what do you think?" she asked. Her father, struggling with his judicial tie, looked down at her.

"What do I think?"

"Yeah. What do you think about her? She's very nice. An' she shouldn't go to this thing by herself. 'Specially 'cos you're goin' alone too."

"You're right, Penny," he said. "Yes, indeed."

"Then I'll go right ahead," his daughter said as she reached for the door.

"Yes," he said to the door, already closing in his face. What have I agreed to now? he asked himself. I think I agreed to ask Rose Chase to go to the MADD dinner-dance with me. There was something to do with the radio station, I think? There can't be anything wrong with that, can there? I'll give Penny a little surprise.

He picked up the telephone, consulted the book, and dialed the number listed for the radio station. When the program director was found Horton said, "This is Sam Horton. I happen to have the morning free today. If you still want that interview I'd be happy to come in. No, I'm available until two o'clock this afternoon. My next free time will probably be in three months. Who will do the interview?"

There was a pause—a very brief pause—then, "Yes, I'd be happy to come by at noon." When he put down the telephone he was grinning. The interviews were usually conducted by Mrs. Rose Chase.

Rose was hot and tired as she finished her walk. The radio station was located on the corner of Elm and Bridge Street, almost exactly in the middle of town. It was a storefront station, located on the ground floor of the Swampscott building. The two studios, one a smaller one for four or five people, the other a twelve by fifteen for audience work, were backed up against each other in the front end of what had once been a J.C. Murdoch dry goods store. Each studio was visible through the plate-glass window of the original store. The tiny control room was tucked carelessly between them, as if it were an afterthought. The whole affair was walled with soundproofing and painted battleship-gray.

Rose brushed by the operations area and walked back into the combined offices, a wide open hall with a scattering of battered desks. The administrative area was still that dingy brown that Murdoch's had left behind when they'd moved out to the Route Six Mall some years previously. Cables and telephone wires had been laid on the floor and then covered with steel conduit, which made walking hazardous. A back corner had been squeezed off to make a pair of tiny offices.

Rose walked down the aisle between the desks. All heads were bent; being busy was always the early morning occupation for Mondays. She dragged her feet into her own little telephone-booth office and sank into the ancient swivel chair which had been her father's. The station's secretary trailed her.

"Anything?" Rose asked as she shucked off her suit coat and hung it over the back of her chair.

"Just the usual," Alice Trent said, looking at a list on the clipboard in her hands. "The licensing board has a new schedule out."

There was a moment of silence. Rose looked up. Alice was the nervous type, and her eyes were glued to Rose's coat. "There's something—your coat is alive!"

Startled, Rose turned to look before she remembered. "Ah! Nothing important. Kittens. And maybe I'd better take them out before—"

A penetrating smell wafted across the office. An ammonia smell. "See if you can find me a cardboard box," Rose pleaded. "Quick!" Her hand dove into the nearest pocket and was welcomed by a rough little tongue. A happy tongue in a dry pocket. "There's a good little darlin'," she murmured as she stooped and set the animal on its feet on the floor. It wobbled a moment on the highly polished linoleum and began to chase its shadow across a beam of sunlight.

The other kitten was crying. In the middle of a wet pocket, unhappy. Cats had a fanatic interest in cleanliness. Rose snatched her out—him out—and tried to comfort him, but to no avail. Alice came thundering back with an old paper carton and some loose newspapers.

"Crumple up the paper and put it in the bottom of the— Where the devil is that other one?" Alice set the box down and one kitten was dropped into it. It seemed to be just what he wanted. He scrabbled around a little bit and then lay down.

"The other one is under the radiator," her secretary said mournfully, "and it's too late because she did, too."

"Well, at least she waited until she was out of my pocket." Rose tried to sound grateful, but it was a hard task. She sank to her hands and knees and fished under the radiator. Her skirt crept up. With one hand she felt for the kitten, with the other for the hem of her skirt.

Rose's hand closed over the refugee kitten. She tried to back out from under there gracefully, but her skirt was not cooperating. "Why me?" she muttered as she snatched up the wandering feline and then crawled not too gracefully to the kitten box.

Rose took a moment to soothe the kitten, then placed it gently in the box with its twin. They greeted each other as if the separation had been of years, not minutes.

"I see that you're busy with the gift I gave you yesterday," the deep voice behind her said gently. He wasn't hard to place. Sam Horton.

"Please," she said with a small smile, looking up at him, "I'm proof positive of the results of your give-away love." She took a deep, explanatory breath. "Can't you smell it?"

After taking a big gulp of air, Sam smiled down at her and said, "I thought I gave you kittens, not skunks. Wouldn't it be just like a cat to go and change species on you?"

"It's not their fault," she was quick to respond. "I admit I forgot I put them in my pockets. And unfortunately they were quick to remind me—when I wasn't quick enough to correct the error. The dry cleaner will be overjoyed to clean my jacket."

"Yeah, sure," he commented laconically. He was enjoying his view of her legs. His eyes were so busy that his brain had disconnected. They weren't the longest legs he'd ever seen but for their length they were prime.

Rose suddenly became aware of his stare and the amount of leg she was showing. Time to stand up, girl, and pull down your skirt, she yelled at herself. "Excuse me for a moment." She tried to stand up, but up was blocked—by Sam, a smile on his face as he leaned over her with his hand outstretched. She hesitantly put her hand in his and he pulled her to her feet easily. But he didn't stop when she was on her feet. He pulled her into his open arms. They stood for a moment in each other's embrace. She felt comfortable and a little daring; he felt as if he'd spent most of his thirty-four years waiting for Rose Mary Chase to come into his life.

Alice came back to the office with the station's janitor trailing behind her. "Under the radiator, Harry," Alice directed as she led him in.

It got very close in the cubbyhole Rose called an office. "Perhaps," Alice continued, turning to face Rosie and Sam, "we could clean up in here more easily if you two could go somewhere else..."

"Yes, ma'am," Sam said. "Why don't we just move on out of this room? And go, say, over to the church across the street."

"What exactly would we be praying for, Mr. Horton?" Rosie's curiosity was aroused. What would he say next?

"Well," he said very seriously, "I thought we might pray for better understanding between us and patience for the interview you're scheduled to do with me this afternoon. Or maybe we could just take a few minutes to get married?"

One of the kittens was still crying. Rosie bent to pick it up. She cherished the animal at her shoulder and glared at him. A likely story, she told herself. Run across the street and get married! He stood in the narrow doorway and smiled as she offered him the still crying kitten. He backed away hastily.

"Me, I have allergies," he said. "Cat allergies."

"Well, look, Mr. Horton," she said, "you could always get an allergy pill—"

"You'll pardon us," Alice interrupted. Horton looked at her blankly. Rose looked at her, puzzled. Horton didn't know the problem and Rose had forgotten the solution in the rush of blood to her head. "We can't get out unless one of you—or both—moves into the outer office."

Sam Horton grinned at Rose and stepped backwards, almost falling over the newsman who had come to see what the teletype circuit had to say. Rose cocked her head and studied Sam for a second or two. No two ways about it, she told herself. I don't want to fool around with *this* man. Not on my life!

Sam watched Rose—little Rosie?—out of the corner of his eye. Lord, he told himself, I'd sure like to fool around with *this* woman! And even my daughter approves, I think. Of her, not of my fooling around!

Thoughts about his daughter drew his attention to one of the battered desks at the front of the bullpen. A group of teenagers was gathered around the desk, while the man behind it made some effort to establish order. And sure enough one of the participants, juggling her electric wheelchair as if it were a calico pony, was his daughter Penny.

"Who's that man?" Sam Horton asked in the suspicious voice of a guardian father.

Rose came out of the office to his side. "That's Henry Fowler," she told him. "He's our daytime disc jockey." A small pause. "And our program director." Another pause. "And our chief salesman. I have a guilty conscience every time I think about him. We don't pay him enough."

"So give him a raise."

"Hey, for that you have to have money. This station is being held together by old friends and chewing gum."

"A man of great import, huh?"

"He likes rock music. That's why we have all these crazy rock programs," Rose muttered. "It's a good idea, this encouraging the kids to visit. And look who leads the list. Penelope Horton, of course."

"I saw," he said softly. "We've both arrived at the same place, working from different needs. Penny loves modern rock. And I understand you need an escort to the MADD benefit dinner. My daughter has sold you a ticket?"

"Dutch treat? I really don't need a partner," Rose said, pulling back away from him and his hypnotic smile. "I'm a member of the committee."

"I could still escort you," Sam said with a cajoling smile. "I don't know anyone around here and I'd hate to go alone to a dinner for a charity I fully endorse."

"Well," she drawled, "we'd have to go early. Is that Penny's problem? A drunk driver?"

"No," Sam said, looking over at his daughter who was all bright smiles and plenty of questions. "She suffers from a birth defect. Her doctor assures us that with just one more operation she'll be able to walk. There are days when she is the bravest person I know. But back to the subject—will you please come to this dinner-dance with me on Saturday week?"

"Saturday week?" Rose said, startled. "I thought there'd be more time."

"More time?" Sam smiled knowingly down at her. "More time to think up an excuse not to go? Sorry, but the benefit is next week on Saturday and Penny will be severely upset if you don't go."

He must have taken lessons from Millie, Rose thought. He seems to know instinctively which of my buttons to push.

"All right," she said. "I'd be overwhelmed to attend this formal affair with you." Now, she thought, say something to get off the subject.

When no response came from him she continued, "I take it that while Penny may enjoy modern rock Dad does not?"

"My days of rock and roll ended with the Beatles."

"The Fab Four? At least, that's what I've been told they were called. You realize, of course, that your comment instantly dates you?"

"I have an excellent memory," he stated grandly, "and I don't consider myself to be old." He stood there looking down his nose at her while she tried not to laugh in his face.

Good Lord, he thought, I just look at her and I have these lustful thoughts. I can picture her in my bed, on a blanket in a green field, in a black silk negligee... Most of all, I can see her in my arms.

"To hell with it," he murmured as he pulled her up close to him. She started to fight, and then gave it up and collapsed against him. Her eyes flared in alarm and then half closed in a sleepy sort of retreat. And then he did it.

It might have been a decade later that he finally broke off the action and allowed her to come up for air. Her little frame shivered, as if she had been thrown into ice water. She panted for breath, and then settled back against him, clinging to his arms.

"Rosie, what are you doing this afternoon?" he asked gently. She stumbled back from him, back into her little office, and almost fell into her chair. I've been kissed right in the middle of my office, she recalled dreamily. If my dad were still here he'd be shouting something stupid at me, like "Not during business hours, Rose!"

"What exactly are you here for, Mr Horton?" Rose asked breathlessly.

"What are you doing this afternoon?"

"I don't really know," she told him. "Why do you ask?"

"Because I did mention that we might go over to the—"

"I—I don't know," she gasped. "Is this where I say, Oh, but this is so sudden?" And it was. Too sudden! She forced herself to control her breathing, then took another minute to smooth down her skirt and blouse. "I've *been* married, Mr. Horton," she said, straightening her back, "and I don't plan to get married again."

The electric wheelchair was practically silent, but Rose could feel that Penny was there with them. "What are you two doing?" The girl whirled her chair around in front of them and braked.

"Nothing much," her father told her. "I just asked Rose to marry me, and she's stuttering, so I guess that means not at this time, Penny."

"Well," the little girl said, "maybe she's not feeling well, or doesn't ever want to get married on Mondays, or is planning to rob the First National Bank— Daddy, you're some kind of a clod. You really are. Is that the way you proposed to Mama? Whatever happened to the romancing and wining and dining and stuff like that? Rose is a nice lady, and I like her a lot."

"So you think I should try again?"

"Of course. Kiss her again, why don't you?"

"I'll do that."

"Wait—wait just a minute," Rose objected.

"Now what? You don't want to be kissed again?"

Rose tried for one more deep breath, and managed to quiet her shaky nerves. "I don't mind the kissing, but I've got a radio station to run."

Sam Horton bent over and snatched up the kitten which had escaped from the box. Penny opened both her arms and welcomed the little tyke. "I love kittens," she said. "In fact, my cat gave birth to two kittens a little time ago." She took a moment and picked up the second kitten, which had started to cry without his sister, and stared at it. The grin faded from the child's face.

"Oh, Daddy! You gave my kittens away! That's hateful!" The girl dropped the kitten into her lap, gunned the electric wheelchair in a circle, and headed for the front door. "And you needn't come by for a ticket for that dance! I'm sure they don't allow pet-stealers in! You ought to be ashamed of yourself! Both of you!"

Quiet weighed down the atmosphere until Penny slammed out the door and it crashed to behind her. Rose stepped away from him and looked up. "You didn't tell her?"

"I—er—forgot."

"What a wonderful father you are," Rose said sarcastically. "I suppose you abuse the child in other ways as well?"

"Now just wait a damn minute," Horton roared. "I—"

"Are you ready for that interview?" the station manager asked as he joined them.

"No interviews today," Rose yelled at the pair of them as she walked back into her little closet of an office and slammed the door behind her.

"Some days," the disc jockey murmured, "you can't make a nickel around here."

CHAPTER THREE

ROSE managed to drag herself home on Saturday week, late in the afternoon. The sultry heat had boiled away the sunshine in her cheeks, and even her canary-yellow sundress appeared faded. Millie was waiting for her at the front door, a doleful expression on her usually bright face.

"Don't tell me," Rose submitted. "The President died?"

Millie shook her head. "Worse."

"The Red Sox have fallen into last place?"

"Worse."

"Nothing could be worse than that," Rose insisted as she started up the stairs, dropping a piece of clothing on each step. "You'd better tell me."

"Mr. Horton."

"Oh. Him!" There was a brief pause. She stopped on the stair. "So don't leave me abandoned. Him what?"

"He came by. His daughter demands that we return her other kitten, or else—"

"Or else?"

"Or else she'll sue us. Now that we have a lawyer in residence in the town she figures she can get a good price, him being her father and all. So what do we do?"

"Oh, Lord," Rose said, sighing. "I guess there's nothing we can do but give it back. A cute little fellow, but—"

"I'm glad you said that," Millie commented, "because I did."

"You—!" She shook her head back and forth slowly and went back to her stair-climbing, also slowly.

"You aren't mad?"

"No, I'm not mad, Millie, but since you've already done the deed I wish you wouldn't ask me to make a decision." Millie was bound to have something else to say, so Rose shut the bathroom door behind her and turned on the hot-water spigot.

There was, thank God, plenty of hot water. Steam cloaked the tiles inset on the wall and beclouded the windows. Rose disrobed at leisure and then stuck a toe into the tub to test the temperature. Too hot! She snatched her foot back with a little squeak of alarm. At least she thought she squeaked. A knock thundered on the door and the squeak was repeated—from outside in the hall.

"Now what?" Rose inched the door open and peeked around the sill.

Millie was standing outside, a tiny black cat in her hand.

"He came back," she announced. "For the third time."

The kitten grumbled at her, then wiggled free and jumped onto Rosie's bare shoulder. The tiny claws penetrated. Rose yelled and moved out into the hall.

"There now," Millie said.

"'There now' nonsense," Rose complained, rubbing her shoulder in anguish. "How did he get in?"

"The front door," Millie said. "The wind keeps blowing it open."

The pair of them looked at each other and sighed. The front doorbell rang with a mighty peal, and a deep bass voice called, "Anybody home?" Footsteps moved toward the bottom of the stairs.

"No," Millie yelled. The kitten mewed and scrambled higher into Rosie's cap of curls. Heavy feet clumped up the stairs.

"No," Millie yelled again. "Nobody's home. We're not—"

But by that time he was high enough up the stairs to see for himself what she was not.

"Oh, you're not—"

The bathroom door slammed shut behind her as Rose dashed back into sanctuary. "Go away," she yelled through the closed door.

"Oh, you're—"

"Naked," Millie said firmly. "Back down stairs, boy-o."

"But she has the kitten," he said. "My daughter's threatening to run away from home if I don't get the kitten back today!"

"You should be so lucky," Rose yelled. "Go pack a bag for her. Tell her not to cross the highways!"

"Not very sympathetic," he responded dolefully. "I love the kid. Come on out!"

Footsteps stuttered on the stairs as Millie herded him back down to the living room. "But I have to have that—" His voice faded as the kitchen door slammed shut behind him.

Rose plucked the kitten out of her hair and tickled its plump little stomach before she set it down on the rug. "What to do?" The kitten wiggled sympathetically.

"Oh? You have trouble with him too?" Rose leaned over to check the temperature of the water, sweeping the kitten up with one hand, unthinking. The cat sensed the water, squalled, and leaped for the floor, backing into a corner.

"Hey, I'm sorry." She really was. The water had somehow cooled more quickly than the animal's friendship. Rose sneaked over to the bathroom door and edged it ajar. Nothing could be heard from downstairs.

"Well, he's gone." Rose chortled. The kitten laughed outright. "Don't be a smart—!" And don't say things like that, she chided herself as she reached back behind the bathroom door and snatched one of her old robes from off the hook.

Old was hardly the word for that robe. She struggled into it, finding three arm holes where only two should be. She was halfway down the stairs before she managed to get the belt knotted. And stopped dead in her tracks as the kitten let loose an undignified roar. Going up was no problem for kittens; coming down was a dead loser! Rose leaned backwards and scooped up the little animal.

Downstairs seemed empty. "Millie?"

"In the kitchen."

Rose tickled the kitten under his chin and backed her way through the kitchen door. "I'm glad you got rid of—" she said, and then turned around and swallowed her tongue. He was sitting at the kitchen table, a gleam in his eye that scared her.

"Ah. There you are," he said. "Did you notice that your robe is untied?" She stared at him, both hands frozen in place, hypnotized. He was licking his lips, and there was a hungry look on his face.

A cool breeze touched her breast, reminding her of how little she was wearing. She gulped and dropped the cat. It meowed as it found its legs before it hit the tabletop, and then dodged Sam's sweeping hand as it jumped down to the floor.

"Damn," he said.

Rose used both hands to close her cleavage. "Indian giver," she snarled.

"And what's that supposed to mean?"

"An old New England phrase," Millie interjected. "And not the least bit true. It relates to people who give gifts and then demand them back."

"Your cat's on the floor," Rose said stiffly. "Kindly take the animal and leave my premises."

"Help me catch the damn thing," he pleaded.

"Not me," Rose said.

"I can't hear a thing," Millie said as he stumbled over her feet.

"It's my daughter's cat, not mine," he grumbled as he dived under the table and bumped his head on its solid oak undersurface.

"What a lovely stepdaughter she'll make," Rose said sarcastically.

He came up for air, cat in hand and a fierce glare on his face. "Some day you'll be sorry you said that." He was a big but graceful man. He glided to his feet and tucked the little beast in his coat pocket.

"You may be sorry right now that you did *that*," she counseled him. "He has a bad habit when carried in coat pockets!"

"Beeswax," he growled, and headed for the door. The light aluminum screen slammed behind him.

"Beeswax?" Rose asked.

"Another old New England saying," Millie quipped.

"But I'm not an old New Englander," Rose said, sighing. "See if you can get a carpenter to come tomorrow and fix that door."

The cab came for her promptly at six-thirty. Only at times like this did Rose miss her own automobile. She had two of them, for a fact, in storage up in New Bedford, but didn't trust herself driving. Not since Frank died. There were too many drivers in Padanaram, each claiming the sacrosanct right of passage down the middle of the street.

And besides, parking was a problem; there seldom was a parking space to be found anywhere in the village.

"Watch your skirt," Millie said for the umpteenth time. Rose smiled, and tugged her ankle-length pencil-thin blue skirt carefully around her. Luminescent blue, for a fact, sparkling in the evening sunset. The dress had a transparent lace neckline, tightly shaped just below her breasts in the old Empire style, setting off her mother's pearls. A hobble skirt that made dancing an adventure. Rose loved adventures.

"Perfect," Millie said, sighing. "Be careful. Come home early. Don't smoke or swear. Behave yourself."

"That's just what you said at my high-school prom. In other words, don't have any fun?"

"Oh, you!"

"I'll look after her," Pete Wilkins said. There was only one taxi in the village; Pete was it's only driver. He was a big bruiser, a former marine sergeant who would indeed look after her. The old cab glided down Summer Street carefully.

"Westfall Country Club, Miss Rose?"

"Where else?" Rose commented as she settled back in the seat. "Sometimes I wish there was—"

"There will be," Pete said. "Some day."

Yes, Rose thought. Some day. Some day my prince may come. Sam Horton? A great broth of a man. Handsome. Too bad his daughter doesn't like me. Those kittens got us all off on the wrong foot, didn't they? But that was all *his* fault, giving them away without the child's permission. What a rotten father. But on the other hand, she ruminated, he's some sort of a bull moose, isn't he? Muscles on top of muscles, a handsome, square-cut face, thick, flowing black hair—!

"And here I am going to the dance without a date," she muttered.

"Oh, we're already here," Pete told her as he pulled the cab in under the canopy at the country club. There were a couple of drops of rain. "How come you've come so early?" he probed.

"I'm chairperson of the ticket committee," Rose answered. "Chairlady? Chairman?"

Pete pulled up under the white marquee and came around to help her out. "I'll be parked right over there," he said, pointing to the corner of the dark parking lot. "Be careful in that skirt. Millie will kill me if you get grease on that—"

"I won't blame you," Rose said. "I'll tell her we were mugged, or something like that."

"Nobody here is gonna mug you," Pete declared. "They wouldn't think of it!"

"No, they wouldn't," Rose said, sighing. Nobody would think of it, would they? Isn't that an awful thing to say? Almost thirty, as quiet as a church mouse, and nobody would even *think* of molesting me!

She fumbled around in her mouth for a pleasant smile, and finally found one as she climbed the four steps up to the double glass doors. There was a subdued clatter from inside. The doorman held the doors wide for her.

"You're almost the first one here," he said. "Except for—"

"Rosie!"

Rose ducked her neck down into her collarbone. She didn't have to look to identify him. "Chad," she said cautiously. "Chad Westbrook!"

"Right the first time," he boomed. Rose shivered. Chad Westbrook. A hail-fellow-well-met sort of guy. Taller than most any other man in Padanaram, at six feet six. He had once rowed on the Crimson eight at Harvard, or so he said. A few people had difficulty remembering what it was he had done since then. But Rose knew; he handled some of her investment accounts, and wanted to handle more, but Rose held back. She could still remember her uncle Ralph's warning about dog training.

"First," her uncle had said, "you have to be smarter than the dog." And Rose was never quite sure that Chad was smarter than her investment portfolio.

"You're early, Chad."

"Early bird and all that," he said. "I played nine holes with the president of the National Bank, so I figured to just come into the clubhouse and see who I could catch."

Whom? Rose asked herself. He took her arm in his typical football grip. "Thought any more about turning over more of your accounts to me?"

"No, I haven't had the time," she gasped as she tried to shake off his grip. "And I'm the ticket committee tonight and I have to get organized."

"Sometimes I think you're trying to avoid me," he said mournfully.

"Who, me?" She managed to get her arm free, and hurried over to the two young people who would be manning the door for tonight. It was hard to hide one person among two others, but Rose was getting accustomed to trying. Besides, Chad was wearing a diamanté rose bow tie, and facing that took more courage than she could muster. The five-piece local band was warming up. Would-be dancers were about to be done good to. Little Rose took a deep breath and plunged into the fray.

By eight-thirty the diners had been seated, and Rose found her own place, thankful that Chad Westbrook was three seats down on the opposite side of the table.

For some reason the chair to Rose's left was empty. She puzzled at it for a moment. All the tickets had been sold. A cool breeze rattled at the French windows and sent a shiver up Rose's spine. Somewhere, tucked into her tiny purse, was a filmy silk shawl. She took it out and draped it over her shoulders.

Noise took command of the room; thunder roared outside on the terrace as a storm pranced over the hills from Russel's Mills. Dishes clattered, conversations sparkled, hurrying waiters conferred. There was an occasional pause. Rose turned to the diner on her right, took a deep breath, and said, "And how are your roses doing, Mrs. Rappaport?"

Of course with Sadie Rappaport that was all the conversational start required. Rose leaned back in her chair and let the one-way conversation flow over her. Mrs. Rappaport grew the finest roses in the village, and was not above telling anyone about it, in some detail, at the drop of a hat. Rose struggled with a yawn.

"Not too polite, that," the deep voice murmured in her ear. Rose snapped to attention.

"You!"

"I believe so."

"How did you get in here?"

"I'm intensely interested in MADD," he said. "So I bought a ticket."

"And left Penny alone in this kind of weather?"

"Not exactly." He scraped his chair a few inches closer. "What is it with you? You're always trying to make me out to be a terrible father. You'll remember that just a few minutes ago this weather wasn't this sort of weather."

"Sophist!" she muttered at him. "I'm not making you out to be anything. You are what you are, and I call them the way I see them!"

"Thank you, lady. I'm just overwhelmed by the kindness of your heart. I might not have come if you hadn't invited me."

"Me? Invite you?"

"In my very daughter's hearing, Rose Mary."

"Don't call me that."

"Look." She waved across the room. "On table number four there's an empty seat. That invitation was long since canceled. Why don't you—?"

"Hush," he commanded. Rose's mouth came to a full stop, half-open. It wasn't often in the village that anyone tried successfully to silence Rose Chase. She sputtered at him, and half rose from her chair. Somehow or other an arm dropped across her shoulders and pinned her to her seat. Her mouth tried to form a few dozen words of reprimand, only to find his mouth at her ear.

"Hush now, Rosie. The chairwoman wants a word or two." And to make sure she left room for the chairwoman his lips coursed down from her ear and sealed off her mouth.

She struggled for a moment or two. Her lips were overwhelmed. She tried to evade him, but his weight and muscles kept her pinned down. And besides, all this kissing business was doing something to her mind. She gave one more wiggle, and then collapsed into her chair.

"And she grows some fine roses too," Sadie Rappaport said. "The speaker, I mean. Oh, you've got something in your eye, Rose? Here, let me help."

"I can take care of my fiancée," Sam Horton said genially. "Had lots of practice, you know."

"Well, I never," Sadie said. And since she was the leading gossip in the village she moved back an inch or two to take notes. "Fiancée? I didn't notice the ring. How long have—?"

"Hush," Sam Horton said. And since any serious gossip knew when to listen Sadie Rappaport did just that.

"Well, you can't hush me," Rose told him firmly.

"You'd better believe I can," he threatened.

"Dictator! I say what I like when I like it, and I am *not* your—"

She managed another second's worth of splutter until his lips shut her down again.

"And I'll—" she squealed as he came up for air, and then sealed her off again. She struggled pro forma; he lifted her off her chair.

"Well, really," the speaker interjected, but she was smiling all the way as she stepped back from the podium. "Have I talked enough? Shall we dance?" A scattering of applause rose to a swell of congratulations; Rose Chase was well liked in the village and all eyes were on her.

The membership made get-up-and-dance noises, punctuated by the incessant crashing of the thunder. Rose was still trapped. Then Sam stood up, taking her with him, her feet some six inches off the floor. The band made music noises something in the order of "Hail To the Chief"—somewhat overdoing it in a village of Padanaram's size.

Chairs scraped and couples formed up for the dancing. Ballroom dancing, that was. The village did not go in much for line-dancing, or anything more sophisticated. And Rose was still six inches up in the air. Couples whirled by them, offering either a titter or a congratulation. Sam lowered Rose's feet to the floor just as the band ran out of breath. As Rose did too.

"There," he said with a large amount of satisfaction in his voice.

"There?" Rose took in three deep breaths. "Now why would you want to say a stupid thing like that?"

He held her close, peering into the depths of her startling green eyes. "Why, it seemed like the thing to do," he said in an absent-minded tone of voice. He leaned forward and nuzzled her nose.

By that time Rose had managed to work up a good head of steam. "Damned if it was," she spat out. "It was the worst time and the worst place and the worst subject you could have mentioned. And you're the—''

"I understand," he said, chuckling. "I'm the worst—''

"You said it, not me," Rose returned. "My mother taught me never to say too much of the truth."

"But—''

"But nothing, Mr. Horton," she said fiercely. "Your daughter hates me. I am not about to become the Wicked Stepmother just for your amusement. Not about to. Got that?''

"But—''

"Think," she snarled. "Kittens. Kittennapping. Anger! Turn me loose!''

His arms loosened reluctantly. Rose shook herself like a puppy breaking out of water and stepped back a half-pace.

"Penny could get over that," he suggested hesitantly.

"Well, I couldn't," Rose said as she swung her open right hand and slapped the handsome side of his face. "See?''

They were gathering a crowd again. The band struck up some impromptu wrestling music. Rose whirled around in a circle, her face blush-red. "Now see what you've done," she said, snarling. "You're making me into a conspicuous fool!''

"Me? What the devil have *I* done?" he demanded to know. "One little kiss—''

"*Little*?''

"So maybe medium-sized." He stopped to tug down the hem of his cummerbund and straighten his tie. "I forgot how small you are, lady. On an ordinary woman of your age it would hardly have been a nose-twitch. And for that I get a raucous lecture, a slap in the face, and an accusation about me and my daughter that's right out of the clear blue sky! If I had my office open I'd be suing you for every penny you own!''

Rose doubled her hands up into fists and managed to freeze them into position. "If I had my druthers . . ." she hissed.

"I know," he returned. "Death and destruction. But tell me, just what made you think I was offering to make you my daughter's stepmother? As I think back over the evening I can't for the life of me remember when there was any discussion about home and marriage and stepmothering."

Her doubled hands came up to her cheeks, but there was not enough fist in either to cover the state of her embarrassment. Think back, Rose Chase. Stepmother? Had he said a word about that? Or had she, in her usual haste, managed to put the cart before the horse again?

The band switched to a waltz, a hard number to play with only two guitars, a set of trap-drums, a banjo and a half-hearted trumpet. But effort could occasionally overcome need. The dancers began to move again in a slow circle around the perimeter of the room. The wind snatched at the double doors, rain smashed down, and the storm marked off a quadrant of the floor for its own. The circling dancers indented their circle and cheered as two husky waiters fought the door shut again.

Sam Horton stepped closer, collecting rainwater on the back of his tuxedo while sheltering her. "Can't think of an answer?" he probed.

"No, I can't," she said defiantly. "But I'll keep trying, and—"

He tugged gently at her hand and pulled her closer. Her chin nestled against the hard muscles of his chest. He tugged again, and pressed his other hand against the small of her back. Unwillingly her head turned, until her cheek was flat against him. He bent slightly, and his chin came down gently into the forest of red hair.

There was a certain peace resulting. Nice, she told herself. Nice indeed. A girl could go a long way before finding a nicer place to— Damn the man! He's hypnotic! She shrugged all over, managing to pry an inch or two away from him.

"Rosie?"

Chad Westbrook, all six feet six of him, was doing his best to break up their little tête-à-tête. He towered over Sam like a steamboat running clearance over a rowboat. He was the sort of man who made familiar noises about twice a day like "fiancée" and "marriage" and "help you control your money" whenever Rose was in sight. Occasionally he had some particular use for a little girl of Rose's size when being overrun by strangers. Like now. Rose Chase switched moods from 'Comfort in the Afternoon' to 'Let's get a little Even in the Evening'. She managed to urge all three of them to a corner of the floor.

"Chad," she said, half out of breath. "I've been looking for you for hours. This is Sam Horton, who has just moved into the village."

The pair of them looked at each other like a pair of pit bulls measuring for a place to bite.

"Sam plans to set up business in the village, Chad. He's a lawyer, and he's looking for office space—and I suppose machines and telephones and things like that— and I told him that although we don't have a real-estate office in town I'm sure you could find him something he might make some use out of. Sam, this is Chad Westbrook, from one of the old-line families in the area." So there, she thought as she stepped back to catch her breath.

The words were compelling to Chad. Like the many widows in the village, Chad was the last of his line—a line which had managed to reach the twentieth century dead broke. Words like "lawyer" and "office" and the implication of money were sweet music to Westbrook's ear. He shifted out of his "pugilist" style.

"Why, I'm sure we could find something useful to you," he boomed as he grabbed Sam Horton's arm and tugged him even further away from the crowd.

Rose settled back on her heels and smiled as she watched the two of them disappear around the corner of the Christmas decorations. "Never to be seen again," she murmured as she turned around ready to make her escape.

"Now I've got you," Sadie Rappaport said as she backed Rosie up against the wall and whipped out her pad. "Tell me everything!"

"I—there's nothing to tell," Rose gasped.

"Fiancée," Sadie prompted.

"Not a word of truth in it," Rose said. "He's a lawyer. Lawyers are often a little loose with the truth."

"You deny it all?"

"Every word. Cross my heart and hope to die."

"There was an awful lot of kissing for a rumor with no truth in it," Sadie murmured.

Rose was still more than a little bit confused. "It wasn't all that awful," she said. "Some of it was—very interesting."

"Aha!"

"What's that mean?" Rose asked, panicking.

"It means there's more to this than meets the eye, Rose Chase."

"I—just remembered something. I have to get home. We have a problem at home."

"We?"

"Millie and I."

"Aha!"

"Don't 'aha' me another 'aha'," Rose begged as she tore her arm out of Sadie's tough-as-leather hold and dashed for the front door. Her cab driver saw her coming, and moved over under the protective canopy.

"Had enough, Miss Rose?"

"Had enough," she agreed, sighing. In minutes he drove her down the hill, across the bridge, and back to Summer Street. By that time the rain had let up and the wind had dropped. A fine mist covered the village and the marina, like a ghost-hand hiding the world.

"Lucky," her driver told her. "Better run!"

"A lot you know," she told him. "Try running in a hobble skirt and see how *you* make out!"

He came around and opened the door for her. "Never tried one of those things in the Marines," he said, chuckling. He moved ahead of her, leaving the cab door open in order to get to her gate, and preceded her down the path to the front door, where he wrestled her for the knob. And then she was inside and breathless.

And there was something on the carpet in the living room. A little black spot that awoke protestingly, mewed happily, and came running for her foot.

"Hush!" Millie came out from the kitchen, shushing her and snapping off the light which Rose had managed to turn on.

"Hush?"

"We have company."

"We have—"

"I've never known you to be so slow," Millie said as she gestured toward the big couch in the corner. Rose blinked. There was a pile of something on the couch, covered by a light blanket. A quiet something.

"Don't tell me," Rose groaned.

"Okay, I won't."

"Don't tell me you won't," she whispered fiercely. "He had the colossal nerve to use us as a baby-sitter?"

"That's the kind of nerve he has," her housekeeper admitted. "But she's no trouble at all, just as long as she thinks nobody is trying to steal her kittens. Besides, you invited him to the dance, and then you walked off before he arrived to pick you up. Some manners, let me tell you. Come out in the kitchen and have a cup of coffee.''

"And I suppose one of us has to sit up until her father comes for her?''

"You're reading off the right sheet of music," Millie agreed. "I'm going to bed now, and—''

"Millie, you can't mean that I'm to sit up half the night *obliging* that—that lawyer?''

"He's not that bad," Millie commented as she headed for the stairs. "Think how bad it would be if he were a used-car salesman!''

CHAPTER FOUR

"SOREHEAD," Millie grumbled as she brushed the breakfast crumbs from the table. Cinderella's ball was over. Another Sunday morning had come. Sunshine dappled the yellow-painted walls of the kitchen. The Hortons, father and daughter, were out in the front yard having a deep conversation. Both the gunmetal-gray kittens were tumbling around in the kitchen, hunting each other.

"But you'll be very careful of my kittens," Penny had solemnly instructed. "This is not a give-away. I promised their mother they'd be home before nightfall." Which had brought an acquiescent nod from Rose.

"A wonderful girl," Millie said now. "Such a careful bargainer. She'll make someone a fine daughter, believe me. And it's up to you to make peace with her!"

"You wouldn't say that if you'd been in the living room this morning," Rose retorted. "Four hours of debate, and never giving an inch! So why should *I* make peace with the girl? I still don't really know what she wants of us!"

Millie struggled vainly to put a lid on her mouth because she *had* been there at the kitchen door all morning, and knew full well what Penny Horton wanted. And Sam Horton as well. "You should make peace with the girl because she's going on thirteen and you're an adult."

"Yeah, she's twelve going on thirty-five. She twists her father around her little finger any time she wants!"

"Humph," Millie commented, and then tried to change the subject. "Did you enjoy the dinner-dance?"

61

"Millie, you wouldn't believe it. The band was outstanding—considering they were mostly high-school kids. The food was good. But that—that man!"

"That man what?"

"He insisted on announcing that I was his fiancée, and then, with sixty people looking on, darned if he didn't kiss me right in the middle of the dance floor. Talk about embarrassing! And then he had the nerve to come here—and stayed overnight—he as well as his daughter!"

"I understand he had some little problem with his house, love. There's a leak in his roof. You, of course, could have turned them both out in the rain, couldn't you?"

"No, I couldn't," Rose said glumly. "I was ready to. Had the words all lined up in my mouth, but I just couldn't do it. And you know something? I didn't even get the conversation around to what's wrong with Penny's legs. Birth defects, he said, but I don't know what that means. She uses an electric wheelchair, and wears those heavy metal braces, but—"

Without thinking, the housekeeper said, "Birth defects."

"What?"

"Birth defects," she repeated. "Malformed hips. She's had three operations in her young life. It may be, with luck, that she'll overcome the major problems some time soon."

"I feel like a fool," Rose commented. "I had no idea. She must suffer a great deal. But there's a hope for her? It's not incurable?"

"There's some small hope. They're running a yearly campaign starting next week looking for financial support. The old March of Dimes program."

"We'll have to get the station behind the drive," Rose commented. "Poor kid. You never stop to think about this sort of trouble in children. How did you find out she had it?''

''When she was over here last Wednesday night. You took her father to church, remember? We had a conversation, she and I.''

''Millie, I did *not* take her father to church. He came along of his own volition. In fact, I was pretty embarrassed. He made some announcement as if he and I were—well, as if we were.'' She scraped back her chair from the table, a massive look of disgust on her face. ''And he doesn't—I asked him to be my lawyer—to do something about finding that hit-and-run driver who killed Frank!''

''Crying, Rose Mary?''

''Cryin' mad,'' she said, sniffling. ''He wouldn't even offer to help, that's what. He won't do anything about...'' Her voice trailed off and she sat there with a vacant expression on her face.

''Wouldn't be a bad thing.'' Millie offered up a huge grin. ''Good-looking, healthy, has a good job—''

''What *are* you talking about?''

''Marriage, of course!''

''Oh, Lord, don't you start in on me with that. Not today. I'm not all that interested in getting married again.'' At least not right now! Or to this man! she thought.

Rose stood, readjusted the straps of her ancient green bikini, and picked up the massive Sunday section of the *Boston Globe*. She peeked out the open front door. Sam Horton had gone; Penny sat dejectedly in her wheelchair. Rose went out and dropped the newspaper beside her ragged canvas lounge chair and sat down. Penny's head came up.

''Mrs. Chase—''

''Call me Rose, dear. Why are you crying?''

''Sometimes I— Sometimes I hurt.''

"Do you say so!" Rose was up and out of her chair in a flash. "Do you have some painkiller pills to take?"

"Yes."

"So why don't you take a couple?"

"They're home."

"Well, that's not much of a problem. I'll take you down and your dad can get them for you, right?"

"He's not home." Deep silence. Rose was gradually getting warmed up.

"He forgot?"

"It's not his fault. There are just too many things to do. He can't do them all, you know!"

"I see." Rose said it but didn't mean it. The child's father had only one massive priority: to take care of his daughter!

"Besides, I need my massage," Penny said. "I had one every other day when we lived in Boston, but now there's just not enough time, and I don't know a masseur in this little place. Do you?"

"As it happens, I do," Rose said. "Close enough to bite your nose. C'mon kid."

She gestured toward the front door of the house. Penny wiped her eyes with a closed fist and steered her chair along behind. "I ain't no kid," she said. There was a little gurgle of relief in her voice.

Millie, having heard a part of the conversation, was at the front door, waiting. "Now what's this all about?" she asked.

"Our neighbor has problems," Rose said. "Pains in her legs and arms. She needs a massage."

"Well, she's come to just the right place," the house-keeper said. "My license is good for another ten years."

"And while you get her ready I'll run down to her own house and find her pills—"

"On the shelf in the bathroom," Penny said. "Percasets."

The screen door slammed behind her as Rose made a mad dash out and up the street.

"Gee, I wish she was in *my* family," Penny said, sighing. "Both of you. Why can't you both join up with my family, and then we'd all have somebody to take care of everybody?"

"Then you're not mad at Rose because of the kittens?"

"Of course not. She loves them—and I love her. Really truly."

"It sounds nice," Millie remarked as she guided the child over to the massive couch in the living room. "Unfortunately there's your father to consider too."

"I know," Penny said. "And I got a plan for him, too, only something's wrong somewhere. Ordinarily I could wind my dad around my left finger, but lately there's something distracting him. It's like he's got something extra-strong on his mind."

"It'll work its way out," Millie promised. She spread a sheet over the couch and patted it. "Slide over here now and we'll see if we can't work something out." They both chuckled at the terrible pun.

Two hours later Millie and Penny moved out to the kitchen. Rose, done up to the neck from the day's difficulties, stretched out on the vacant couch and made only a cursory pass at the front page of the *Globe*. Her head drooped, her eyes closed, and she fell into a dream. The world was filled with the smell of flowers. Then there came a soft, deep voice, whispering in her ear. "Rose Chase? The most beautiful rose in the garden?"

Rose lifted a hand to brush away whatever it was that was tickling her nose. She knew nobody was there—it was all a dream. But it was a persistent dream.

"Rose?"

"Go away," she muttered, and brushed at her itching nose again.

"I'm going to kiss you, Rose."

"No, you're not," she grumbled as she rolled over onto her side. "Dreams don't kiss. Go away."

But dreams *did* kiss. Soft and warm and moist, a kiss worth waiting for. Rose managed to open one eye. "You?"

"As you see. Samuel F. Horton, Esquire, at your service."

She closed her eyes with a snap of her eyebrows that might have raised a wind-storm.

"Are you angry at me, Rose?"

"I'm not angry at you," she stated firmly. "You are beneath my dignity to be angry. Go away and judge a beauty contest or something."

"But I'm doing that right now, and you're the winner."

"On second thoughts you don't have enough experience to judge even a beauty contest."

Her left eye opened to measure the effect of her witty come-back. His handsome face was inches away from her, bland and quiet and not at all perturbed.

"And the only way I'll get the right experience is to make peace between Rose Whatchamacallit and Penny Horton."

"Chase. It's a simple name. Rose Chase. Get it right."

"I've tried. I can't get it right. The best thing to do is to change it. Horton is easier to remember. Rose Horton. I like the sound of it."

"You must be mad. Who in the world would want to marry an unemployed lawyer?"

"I have good prospects," he insisted.

"Poverty-stricken," she declared.

"And until I make a lot of money I needn't darken your door again?"

"Well said!"

"Ah, you're a hard taskmaster, Rose Chase. How am I going to take Millie sailing?"

One eye popped open and stared at him. "First you need a boat."

"I *have* a boat."

"Then you need help. Perhaps Millie. But she hardly knows beans about sailing."

"I *know* that." Exasperation glossed over his friendly tone. "That's why I need Rose Chase. I hear tell that she's one of the premier small-boat sailors in all Padanaram."

"That's true. Now please go away. You've annoyed me enough! On Sunday I relax."

"Does that mean we can't go, Dad?" came a soft, sweet soprano voice at her other elbow. Rose cautiously opened the other eye.

"You can't go sailing, Penny," he said.

And why not? Rose thought. Because she can't swim, idiot. How can she swim with those heavy braces on her legs? And if she can't swim she can't sail safely! Having won the debate, to her regret, Rose shrugged and forced her eyes to close again.

"I don't want to put those braces back on," the child said mournfully. Rose's eyes popped open—both of them. No doubt about it; Penny was sitting in her wheelchair *without her braces*.

The kitchen door opened and Millie came bustling out, carrying a large picnic basket. "Well, I'm ready. Do you think this hat becomes me?"

"The best," Penny said cheerfully. "It makes you look twenty years younger."

"The child has a tongue that'll charm the birds down out of the trees," Millie declared.

"But not good enough to take us sailing," Penny added. "We can't go."

"We can't go?" Millie set the basket down on the floor. It was covered with a light towel that wiggled. Two little black heads peered out from under opposite corners.

"Our driver won't come," Penny replied.

Rose slammed her eyes shut. Everyone in the house, including the kittens, was glaring at her. Silence prevailed until the cats set up a fuss.

"Oh, all right," Rose muttered as she swung her legs off the couch and planted them solidly on the old rug. "Nobody has any interest in *my* needs."

Sam snatched her up in his arms as if she were a doll. "That's right," he said. "Duty! Honor! Service!" And then, in front of the crowd of them, he had the unmitigated gall to kiss her again. It was a delightful sensation, but Rose realized that if she let him get away with it this time there'd be no curbing him! Besides, the neighborhood gossip, Mrs. Moltry, was coming down the street, and stopped to get an eyeful through the open door.

"Put me down," she muttered into his massive chest. He kissed her again. "Put me down," she screeched. "I'll sue you for sexual harassment!"

He grinned down at her. "I know a nice young lawyer, just admitted to the bar. She'll work cheap. Wait a minute while I find her card. It's right here in my coat pocket."

"Put her down, Dad," his daughter ordered. "You're not wearing your coat today."

"Six million dollars," Rose threatened.

He shook his head slowly, and equally slowly set her down. "Rose Chase, you're no fun at all," he said sorrowfully.

"All right, all right," she grumbled at him. "I *said* I'd come. Good afternoon, Mrs. Moltry."

The gossip tutted a couple of times. "Sunday, right in the middle of the village," she commented. "And hardly enough clothing to cover the rules of decency."

"Oh? You mean my bikini? Everyone wears them these days."

"Down on the beach, I presume you mean? And certainly not on the Lord's day!"

"You're losing the game," Millie said. "And besides, the sun's out enough to blister, and redheads don't take kindly to—"

"All right," Rose said, sighing. "You don't have to hit me with a baseball bat to make your point. I'll go change."

"You don't have to change on my account," Sam said innocently. "It certainly looks healthy, exposing your—skin—that way."

"Daddy!" his daughter exclaimed disgustedly.

He had the grace to blush—but never stopped looking as Rose dashed for the stairs. In ten minutes she was back, dressed in a long-sleeved red blouse and a pair of faded blue jeans.

"Better," Millie said, noting but not commenting on the fact that the blouse, shadowed by the sun, was as transparent as stained glass. What made it more interesting to Sam Horton was the realization that little Rose Chase was marvelously well equipped in the physical sense, and hardly ever wore a bra.

"Yes, that's certainly better," he contributed.

Mrs. Moltry, who didn't see all that well without her glasses, smiled in approval. Millie hustled them all out to the Horton van before the old biddy took further notice.

His vehicle was a specially designed gray van with powered loading arms, capable of picking up Penny's wheelchair and locking it into position next to the windows on the far side. Millie climbed in behind her, taking the picnic lunch, and the kittens, along with her. There was plenty of room left in that second seat, and Rose headed straight for it, only to be stopped by Horton's arm.

"Front seat for you, lady." He pushed her not too gently up onto the bench seat that spanned the front of the van's cabin. "Nice?"

"I can't reach the floor," she complained. "The darned truck is designed for tall people and I'm not."

"I *had* noticed," he said with a chuckle. "But then short and well fitted is much preferred over long and skinny."

Rose was not sure she had heard correctly, but hesitated in mixed company to pursue the subject. "Depends on who's looking," she muttered, sotto voce.

"Did you know I have exceptional hearing?" he asked. It was Rose's turn to blush.

"Left on Elm Street," she ordered grimly. "The yacht club is just past the bridge."

It was a short drive, but he went slowly, giving Rose time enough to examine him from top to bottom. A big man. Not basketball tall, but certainly blacksmith wide. His square face seemed to be much better-looking than it had on the day they first met, and his eyes were definitely brown. Or maybe dark blue? Like his voice, his eyes were hypnotic. She pulled away from him and stared at the familiar streets coasting by.

He was dressed for sailing: lightweight white duck trousers, immaculately pressed, a cable-knit white sweater that had seen better days, a pair of well-worn sneakers, a Boston Red Sox baseball cap with a long bill to shade his irregular nose. And he beamed energy.

"Hey!"

He jammed on the brakes and turned to look at her. She hadn't fastened her seat belt, and she slid forward against the glove compartment.

"Hey what?"

"You just drove by the entrance to the marina," she said, trying to catch her breath. He was too big to antagonize, so she made herself sound as demure as she knew how. From the back seat Millie, who knew fakery when she heard it, had trouble coughing.

"Oh, that." He reversed smoothly and pulled into the parking lot. The place was crowded, as was usual on a hot Sunday afternoon in August, but he managed to find a parking space near the water. Rose looked up at him in awe.

"I could drive in here a thousand times and never once find a parking space," she said.

"Oh? I never have any trouble." He shut off the air-conditioning. The temperature inside the van immediately shot skyward. Millie climbed out onto the bubbling tarmac. Sam flipped a switch and the automatic loader swung Penny down to the ground as if she and her chair weighed hardly more than a feather. Even machinery is on his side, Rose noted as she slid cautiously out of the high seat. Truly a man to be wary of!

The miracle continued. The dockmaster himself came out of the shade and welcomed him. "Glad you made it, Sam. I put the run-about in slip one, right ahead of you. And I'm glad to see you brought Rose with you. We won't have a thing to worry about, what with Rose aboard. Girl knows every rock and shoal and buoy in the area. The tank's been topped off for you, Rose. Don't wander too far. The weather bureau is predicting fog in another hour or two."

"Rosie the Perfect," he murmured as he came by her.

"You darn well better believe it," she returned as she fell in behind the procession. He led off, plucking Penny out of her chair and carrying her off as if she were no burden at all. Millie followed. Both kittens had their noses out from under the towel by now, enjoying the ride.

And me bringing up the rear, Rose told herself. As usual. It doesn't pay to be short! What am I doing here anyway? I swore that I'd have nothing to do with this man, and look at me, padding along like a house pet! Last night I had a dream—or a nightmare, perhaps. I tried to remember my husband, and I couldn't recall his face! What's happening to me?

"Come on, daydreamer." That rich baritone voice again, which seemed to climb up and down her frame, touching her everywhere. An unfair advantage, if ever she heard one.

"I'm coming," she complained. "What now?"

"Somebody has to get into the boat so I can pass Penny down."

"Somebody? Me?"

"It seems logical."

"To you, maybe. Just remember, your daughter is almost as big as I am and—"

"Stop fighting the bit, Rosie. Get in the boat!"

"I'm getting, I'm getting," Rose mumbled. "And don't call me Rosie!"

The craft was an inboard Speedster, about thirty feet long, with an open well aft, a cabin built forward, and a flying bridge built over the roof of the cabin. The highly polished wood gleamed of polished mahogany, and the fittings were all sparkling yellow brass. A good many muscles had been stretched to maintain the craft in its present condition. Rose, who usually provided that muscle, offered a little bow. Nobody was looking. The name on the stern was *Seaspray—Padanaram*. It looked very familiar. In fact, her crowded mind realized, it was her own craft!

"Well, have you seen enough?" What a hateful voice that could be, Rose thought. Dictator Horton. I wonder where he parks his tumbrel? "The boat," she muttered. "What's going on here? It happens to be *my* boat!"

"Yes, well you can't expect me to bring a run-about all the way down from Boston, can you? So I called Millie and she offered me the use of this one. Nice, isn't it?"

"Yes, nice," Rose muttered as she swung down into the cockpit.

"Are you ready for Penny?"

"Yes, I'm ready. Pass her down." He did. Luckily Millie had already boarded and set her basket down. Rose wrapped two hands around Penny's waist, and Millie added another pair of hands. Between them they hauled the girl over to the port side and established her on the plush bench seat that ran in a U shape around the cockpit. The boat shivered as Sam Horton vaulted aboard.

"All right, slave," he said as he brushed by Rose. "Man the oars."

"This doesn't have oars," she said firmly. "And you're the only man aboard. This is a motor boat. Say after me: *motor boat*."

He gave her a wicked grin. His daughter chanted, "Motor boat, motor boat," as Millie helped her into her orange life vest.

"Motor boat," he agreed. "Motor boat."

Determined to humble him, Rose climbed the portside ladder up to the flying bridge and made her visual checks. Everything was satisfactory, so she started the four-cylinder motor. When it purred at her, and the gauges all showed ready, she leaned over and yelled down at him, "Cast off the bow line."

He hesitated for a moment, consulted with his daughter, and then dashed forward. The wharfinger, a massive grin on his face, uncoiled the line off the bollard and tossed it at Horton. The bow, under the drive of

the choppy waves, began to drift away from the pier.
The stern was still tied up.

"Aft," she yelled at him over the roar of the engine.
"Cast off aft!"

He looked up at her and held a hand cupped to his
ear. The bow of the boat was drifting further away from
the pier, leaving them almost at a right angle, and
pointing them in the general direction of the small sailcraft in the adjacent slip.

"Aft!" she screamed at him. He stared back at her.
Not since her eight-year-old days had Rose felt so frustrated. But the wharfinger, wise to the ways of a million
amateur sailors, had already walked back to the stern,
lifted the aft line off its bollard, and dropped it into the
water. *Seaspray*, free from land at last, drifted grandly
toward the adjacent slip.

"Duck!" Rose yelled, completely confused.

"Clutch," Sam Horton yelled up at her. And with a
shocked expression on her face Sailor Rose engaged the
engine clutch, the propeller began to spin, and *Seaspray*
came out of the slip, leaving just a newspaper page's
width between it and the adjacent expensive sailboat.
For a moment Rose struggled with the wheel, until finally
she brought the bow around to the exit channel out and
away from the marina.

As soon as she could refocus her eyes Rose searched
for Sam Horton. He was still standing on the forward
deck, carefully coiling the bow line. He put it down and
vaulted up onto the roof of the cabin as gracefully as a
trained athlete. Another vaulting jump brought him up
over the side of the windscreen and onto the flying bridge
beside her.

"Well, we did that rather well, didn't we?" he said.

Rose stared at him, her hands still shaking. He wasn't
even breathing deeply. Another score against him!

"Yes," she managed to get out. "Yes, *we* did that rather cleverly, didn't we?" And I hope the coast guard won't take my instructor's license away from me, she thought.

There was some sort of gleam in his eyes that frustrated her. It was as if he was concealing a multiple secret behind the deep brown.

"And now where would you like to go?" she asked diffidently.

"Thataway." He waved an arm southward, down toward where Apponagansett Bay, only a tidal inlet, joined up with Buzzards Bay, the major sheltered waterway that stretched from New York to Cape Cod.

Her cool restored, Rose handled the wheel gently as they moved between the solid rows of small and large sailboats.

"Can't we go faster?" Penny yelled.

"Not on your life," Rose called down. "The yacht club runs races every weekend. And sail has the right of way."

"Well, how about him?" Penny waved an arm toward the mouth of the bay, where a tremendously large motor cruiser was coming in at high speed. So fast that the craft's bow was out of the water, it was riding on the first step in its hull, and a huge rooster-spray was being thrown up on either side of her bow, sending a bow wave out into the anchorage. Rose braced her feet and called down a warning to Millie.

Sam Horton moved closer to her side and wrapped one arm around her narrow waist just as the approaching bow wave struck them. *Seaspray* rocked, climbed a wave or two, and then settled down. She smiled up at him in thanks as she steered out of the path of the speeding boat.

"He looks like a wolf coming down to ravage a flock of sheep," he commented. At just that moment the siren at the harbormaster's office went off with a roar. The speeding boat slowed, came down off its step, and tried to hide itself among the crowds of smaller boats.

"Well, if that's what he is," Rose said, "there's going to be fried wolf for dinner tonight. The harbormaster has police powers in the anchorage."

He grinned down at her and clutched her just a bit tighter. "And you approve of that?"

"Of law? Of course. The harbor is always over-crowded. There's always the chance of a major accident."

"And justice has to be served?"

"Exactly." She was about to say something more when it struck her just where the conversation might be leading. "Exactly," she repeated grimly. "Without fail."

But he refused the gambit. Instead he reached over in front of her and thumbed the toggle switch that turned on the automatic pilot.

"Well, how did you know—?"

He knew more than toggle switches. With the wheel under control he used both hands to turn Rosie around in his direction. "Rosie, girl," he murmured, and before she could take warning he lifted her off her feet and kissed her. It was a warm, simple kiss, and, for all that, exciting. The run-about was still pounding along, bouncing into the waves and shaking the pair of them up and down.

Rose had nothing to say about the whole affair. She was traveling as a subordinate in the ship called love. When he set her down on both feet, instead of following impulse and stepping away, she clung close to his shadow and fought for breath.

"You know a great deal more about boating than you admitted," she charged when she had collected enough oxygen. But there was a gleam in her eye, and a sense of enjoyment crowded her Irish face.

"Not exactly what I expected," he said, chuckling. "But nice. Ever had a kiss like that? I haven't."

"So you've a lot to learn," she chided him. "At my high-school prom I had a boyfriend who insisted on kissing me before we left the house—and I wound up sitting on top of the washing machine, which was running a heavy load. Wow, was he some kisser!"

"I hate that," he grumbled, and pushed his hair back off his forehead. "If you had a lot of boyfriends like that I don't care to hear about them. We'll have to— Whatever happened to him?"

She said, sighing, "He went off, never to be seen again."

His hand remained at her waist, but the pressure softened. They both turned back to the boating business. He flipped off the auto pilot. She put both hands back on the wheel. The gulls who maintained an offshore blockade just off Ricketson's Point began to trail them and dive-bomb their wake, but their ship had nothing to offer.

It was hard to tell whether the increased swells appeared from the water movements in Buzzards Bay, or were just a reflection off the sharp rocks of Mishaum Point. In any event Penny began to turn a delicate green just after they cleared the Point.

"Daddy," she wailed as she sidled closer to the combing, clutching at her stomach. He came down off the flying bridge in one vaulting jump, ending up in the cockpit at the child's side.

"Rose," he yelled up at her accusingly.

"Now what am I to blame for?" Rose muttered as she turned around to look down at the child. A second's inspection told her. She'd had the colossal nerve to let his daughter get seasick!

"I'm going into the shelter of the Slocum river," she called down as she cut the throttle to a whisper and turned north toward the state park. "And Millie has some pills in her little first-aid kit."

"My daughter doesn't take pills without a doctor's prescription," he yelled back up at her angrily.

"Yes, I understand," Rose roared back, just as angry herself. "So let her sit and suffer. I can't turn off the wind *or* the waves." She brushed her hair back to give herself a clear view of the shallow mouth of the river. The rocking of the boat tailed off as the speed dropped. "No pills, no luncheon," Rose yelled at him again. "Let the child suffer because the father's too proud."

"I'm a nurse," Millie coaxed.

"That's not good enough for *my* child," he retorted.

"Gimme the pills," Penny moaned, "or I'm gonna die right here!"

"Give her the pills," Rose roared. "Nobody dies on any ship that I command."

"I don't understand you two," Millie said. "You stand there and argue about something that you know nothing about. Nothing!"

"Millie!" Rose could feel the depth of her housekeeper's disdain. Feel it right through her skin and bones. It cast her into some doubt. Sam Horton she might doubt—and cuss as well, but Millie had been her substitute mother for years. She said hesitantly, "Millie?"

"That's telling her," Sam Horton said. There was a big grin on his face, as if he had just won the battle of Gettysburg.

"And you've got nothing to crow about," Millie told him. "You don't know as much as she does, you big ox. Lord, it would serve you right if she married you and taught you something about children."

"Well!" he snarled.

"Well, hell," Millie said as she fumbled in her purse and pulled out a battered packet. "No pills. There are plenty, of course, Dramamine being one of the earliest."

She pulled out a slip of cardboard, and peeled a little doughnut-shaped tape not more than a quarter of an inch in diameter off it. "But nowadays we modern, educated people use these little bandages that take care of the problem without the child swallowing a pill or taking a hypodermic shot. Now all we need to do is to stick this little plaster just under her ear. Hold your head up, Penny. There. How's that?"

"That's—that's wonderful," Penny said.

"That's only because I've got the boat in quiet waters," Rose said, still trying to defend herself against that monstrous man. "You could spit on her in these waters and cure her mal de mer. You don't need little fake plasters to—"

"Rose Chase," Millie said in a deadly whisper.

"Yes, ma'am," Rose Mary Chase said, and gave up the fight.

The Slocum river was not much as rivers went. Brook it might well have been called further upstream, but here at its mouth it demanded a little respect. The entire east side of the estuary was the Lloyd State Park. School had not yet opened, and the park contained many a child and family picnic. A rickety wharf just opposite *Seaspray* promised enough depth. Her face still blushing from Millie's reprimand, Rose brought the boat gently in, nudged the wharf without bringing it down, then Sam Horton was over the side, busy tying up. His face was as red as hers, although more of it might be blamed on the sun—but not much.

"Serves him damn right," Rose muttered under her breath. "I hope he gets his pants soaked." But he had more skill than she had luck. Glumly she followed the others out onto the wharf, and down to the shaded glen

that made a wonderful picnic area. Penny was recovered
enough to enjoy the meal. The kittens enjoyed it too.
Rose stalked a tree or two away and turned her back on
all of them.

CHAPTER FIVE

AUTUMN came in two days after Labor Day with a cold rush of wind, and Rose was feeling the strain of mental uncertainty as well as bad weather. She was sitting out in her postage-stamp front garden, wrapped in a warm coat, when Millie came out, armed with a tall glass of steaming cocoa. The spoon tinkled as her housekeeper set it down firmly on the wobbly table.

"No news?"

"The paper's full of news," Rosie said glumly.

"I mean from him," Millie insisted.

"Him who?"

"The lawyer man who lives down the block."

"Oh, him!" Rose managed a sip of the cocoa and almost choked. "You forgot the sugar."

"Stop beating about the bush, Rose Chase. I never forget the sugar. You've just become so sour that there's no way I could make the cocoa sweet enough. Here, let me taste." Millie took a hefty slug from Rose's glass, swallowed, and almost turned green.

"I can't believe it," she gasped. "There's no way I could have—" She took four deep breaths. "Now, you were saying about Mr. Horton?"

"So all right, there's no news, and I don't expect any. You know how mad he was when we got back to harbor nearly two weeks ago. You'd think I went out of my way to make his precious daughter seasick! And then we had to radio in for a van to come around the peninsula for his precious little—"

"Ah, Rose Mary."

81

"Well, we did! You and she came back roundabout and I had to bring the boat back with only Sam Horton to help. And that terrible storm came up and I was almost driven ashore. And boy, was he some lousy sailor. But did he care? No sooner did I get a line ashore at the marina than he was over the side and gone, with not a care in the world about me! Not a care! Not a bit!''

"Maybe he was worried about his daughter, Rose. She was not well at all, and I don't mean from being seasick. Rose, in all your life I've never known you to be so unwilling to examine the other side of the story!''

"I don't care,'' Rose said firmly. "You understand? I don't care all that much about him, and if he doesn't wish to—'' She stopped. There was a suspicious gleam of teardrops under her right eye. "Well, I just don't care. I've enough enemies to be concerned about without adding one more.''

"You don't have any as good-looking as he is,'' Millie probed.

"Good-looking I don't need,'' Rose insisted. "I must have caught a summer cold or something. I can't seem to stop my eye from watering!''

She whipped her tiny lace handkerchief out of the pocket of her blouse. "Besides, he's busy.''

"You mean you buried your pride and called him?''

"Business,'' Rose said indignantly. "It was entirely business. That fool Westbrook is suing me and I need a lawyer, only his secretary—''

"Westbrook's?''

"No, Sam's—er—Horton's. She said he's all tied up in an important case—his first one since he came to Padanaram. So he can't—well, you know. Damn it, Millie, don't nag at me.''

"No, I won't nag, love. You could still make friends with Penny, you know. She's been calling every day.''

"You mean coming over?''

"No. On the telephone. She has to put up with him too, you know."

"I—hadn't thought about it that way. You mean she and I—"

"Might make up, except that one of you is a hard-nose down-easter and the other is a confused little girl."

"When you say it that way it makes me sound like the Wicked Witch, doesn't it?"

"You said it, not me."

"Yes." Rosie sighed. But how could one little girl and two black kittens compare to an oversized, oversexed—and how did that get into my train of thought? she thought. Oversexed? Really? She abolished the idea with a regal wave of her hand, and struggled out of her chair.

"There's a lot to what you say, Millie. I'm going to take a walk. I'll bet there's a million things going on in town today."

"In Padanaram? You must be kidding. But a walk would certainly do you some good. You've given up working at the radio station?"

"I should be so lucky. They're getting along fine without me!"

It was seldom that Rose lost her temper with Millie. Her old housekeeper had kept her safe, child and woman, through all her years. But then there had never been such a one as Sam Horton. And just knowing that irritated Rose more than she cared to admit. So she apologized to Millie and steamed down the hill at Bridge Street, elbows pumping, feet making a theoretical two knots, the light offshore wind tussling with her hair, the sweet smell of salt water loosening the gears in her hung-up brain.

She dropped off to idling speed, waving a salute to the guard in the shack at the New Bedford yacht club marina. The guard made no attempt to check her credentials. Everybody in Padanaram who lived on and by the water knew little Rose Chase from childhood. The New Bedford yacht club? The harbor at New Bedford was crowded with anchorages and facilities for the biggest fishing fleet in the nation, and so the yachts and their races had been exiled around to the other side of the Point—to Padanaram.

The harbormaster was out with his glasses, checking for orderly behavior in the anchorage, where some hundred boats of all sizes and shapes made up the club's home fleet.

"Goin' out for a run, Rosie?" he called.

She shook her head. "Just settling my temper," she yelled at him. He waved in acknowledgement. Everyone in the world knew that Rose had a temper. Sometimes good, sometimes bad. This was one of her bad days, when friends took a quick look at the little frown furrows on her forehead and steered clear.

Seaspray, her little runabout, was anchored close inshore, and was receiving all the unwelcome attention of the gulls that haunted the area.

"Damn birds," she muttered as she rounded the end of the slips, planning death and destruction. She was going at full speed, as usual, when she came around the blocked end of slip number three and smashed into the solid figure of—Mr. Sam Horton.

"Aha!" said Sam Horton. "Caught you at last, Mrs. Chase." Behind him Chad Westbrook leaned over Horton's shoulder and grinned at her.

"We've a little business with you," Westbrook declared somberly.

He sounded so belligerent that Rose looked around for some place to run. Horton had his hand on her arm before her feet could respond. "Aha!" he said again, and pulled her to a stop. "Saved ten dollars. Take this."

The paper was a trifold legal device, stamped with a variety of court and county stamps. Rose, still a little confused, looked at him and back at the paper.

"A s-summons?" she stuttered as she flipped through the three pages. "Who?"

"Me," Westbrook said. "My lawyer says I should sue. You've ruined my reputation. And you'd better be ready to settle or I'll take you to court, and I'll seize your radio station and take over the building and the equipment and foreclose your house and put you out on the street, and what do you think of that, Mrs. Chase?"

Rose shook her head gently and tapped the summons on the fingers of her other hand. "To tell the truth I don't rate that very highly, Mr Westbrook. I ruined your reputation? When? How?"

"With your radio station, last Saturday and Sunday."

"My station? What did I say?"

"You know what you said. On that *Behind the Scenes* program. You said that I had swindled Widow McAlister. Swindled, no less."

Her head cocked to one side, Rose studied him. "Well, if I said it it must be true. Only I didn't say it."

"You own the station," Sam said. "So you're responsible for everything said on it. So you get sued, Miss Rose."

"Damn lawyers," she muttered. "You're lucky," she finally said.

"I am lucky?"

"You'd better believe it. I don't have my .357 magnum with me. Otherwise I'd be shooting you. If I said you swindled Addie McAlister I'm sure it's true. And now you want to put me out on the street?"

"My lawyer says he could easily make it worse."

"Ah, you've got a mean lawyer?"

"Even meaner than me, lady. Look at the bottom on the last page."

Rose did. And dropped her purse. The paper was signed, in classical Spencerian, "Samuel F. Horton, Esquire."

"I'll kill him," Rose roared. "And you too, you damn—foreigner!" She scrabbled for her purse. Chad Westbrook dived for the shelter of the yacht club building. Rose Chase came up with her purse in one hand and the index finger of the other extended as if it were a pistol. "Bang! Pow!" she roared. Westbrook squealed as if both shots had hit him dead center, and he fell off the edge of slip number one and into the chill water of the harbor. Sam Horton joined the growing crowd of men who were trying to rescue him.

I knew there was something wrong with that man, Rose told herself. Westbrook, huh! If his family came over on the *Mayflower* they must have been smuggled in!

A car pulled up beside Rose. She turned, and sighed again. One more trouble to surmount.

"Nice shooting," Officer Ramirez called from the police patrol car. "You got a permit to carry that loaded finger?"

Rose Chase, who had never owned a weapon in all her life, lifted her finger up in front of her eyes, then solemnly blew on it as she had seen movie cowboys do.

"No," she said. "No permit. But some day I'm gonna shoot that—that man. Don't say I didn't warn you. Right after I shoot his lawyer!" The pair of them turned to watch as a bedraggled Westbrook scurried down the street on the arm of his lawyer.

"Just like your father," the officer said. "Get in the car." He leaned over and opened the passenger door. "You can't shoot the lawyer. He's the only one in the village."

"You're going to arrest me just—"

"I'm going to buy you a cup of coffee," he said. "That's what we call community policing."

"Yeah, community," Rose said glumly as she sidled into the car. As they drove away, they passed the dripping Westbrook, who shook his fist in her direction. Rather bad-mannered of her, she thought, to wish that he'd get pneumonia. But she wished it on him anyway.

"Now, I suppose," Rose said mournfully, "he will sue me for assault and battery. I threatened him with a hidden weapon—my finger. This is just what I need to make my whole week just jim-dandy."

She was sitting in the police car in front of the Stone Soup, a small take-out restaurant. Police, she thought, must have a hidden sign that opened parking spots for them, even on the busiest streets. "He's going to think that I'm in with the local police and then he'll call on the State Troopers. Could it get any worse? Please, don't tell me it can. I don't want to hear. I'm about to crack up!"

"In the words of my sainted grandmother," the policeman said comfortingly, "'this too shall pass away'." The pair of them sat in the police car and watched as Horton escorted Westbrook into the restaurant, leaving wet footprints on the sidewalk.

"Well, it's the only place open," Ramirez said. Rose looked at him and shrugged.

"Thanks for all your sage advice," she said as she got out of the car. "I'll keep it all in mind."

They walked into the small eatery and both ordered coffee. They had to wait a few minutes while the shop brewed another pot. Rose turned around to look at the customers seated at the few tables available. Chadwick Westbrook and Sam Horton. Were there any greater conspirators in the world? Sitting there dripping at each other and whispering who knew what. Probably a plot to overthrow the government. That miserable son of a cod fish, Mr Samuel F. Horton!

As she watched him talking with great charm and bonhomie to the man whose head she'd wanted on a platter, the anger she'd held in check let go. Almost without thinking she grabbed the ice-water pitcher on the counter and walked over to the table where they sat. Horton's back was to her and he never saw it coming. Most of the customers were watching her with bated breath. Horton and Westbrook were so deep in their conversation that they missed the entire show.

Someone among the customers might have given warning, but they were all local people who'd grown up with Rosie and her temper. Sam Horton was a sitting duck. For a second she debated which one. And then she made up her mind. It felt good to dump the whole pitcher of water, ice and all, slowly over Sam Horton's oh, so charming head. *Yes!*

Then he looked up at her, soaking wet, with his large brown beagle eyes. He appeared so wounded, it gave her a sharp jab of guilty conscience. But only for a moment.

"What did you do that for?" he said quietly, while the whole room strained to hear.

No, she told herself, I don't feel guilty. He deserved it. I hope ice went down his back. Before the guilt could overwhelm her she dropped the glass pitcher on the floor at his feet, turned on her heel and stalked out of the Stone Soup, leaving her coffee, her audience and her victim sitting bewildered.

The customers were stunned because Rosie was not known for letting her words be left unsaid. She normally didn't leave anyone in any doubt as to how she felt on any particular subject. The villagers felt that she was one of the local landmarks. They were proud of her because she would say what most of them might feel but were unable to articulate. Obviously, this was a private battle between the new attorney and Rosie Chase. They'd just have to sit back and wait. Perhaps Mrs. Moltry would know the story. A pitter-patter of applause pursued her out onto the windy sidewalk.

Sam sat in his chair, dripping and confused. "What did I do?" he asked anyone. No one answered; in fact most of the other customers turned back to their own coffee and sandwiches or to their tablemates.

"Looks like you managed to get her angry," Chad grumbled. "I'm going to make sure I never make her annoyed at me—after we settle this suit, of course."

Sam was torn between confusion and anger at Rose and her actions at the café when he left, still soaking wet. He decided to go back to his office and change. He always kept a spare set of clothes there just for emergencies, although this was not one of the emergencies he'd envisioned.

As he slogged across the bridge to his office building he got angrier at Rose for disturbing his first opportunity to get to know Chadwich Byron Westbrook better. The man was definitely slime, but it was going to be difficult to prove. He had charm and old Brahmin blue blood and all the family connections for which one could wish. But—and Sam was sure of this—Chad's hands were dirty. He was living much too well for his salary and his trust fund to support him.

Sam's private investigator, a retired policeman from New Bedford, was waiting for him as he came through the door. Sam's secretary, Veronica, squealed at the sight of him and dashed for a towel from the washroom.

"What happened?" Ruiz Ortega asked.

"What do you damn well think?" Sam muttered.

"Well, if I had the right of it, you fell off the dock— no, here's a half-cube of ice. You dived into a glass of ice water?"

"Funny," Sam grumbled. "Thank you, Veronica."

Veronica had only recently graduated from Dartmouth High School, but she had lived all her life in the village, and knew the entire cast of characters.

"You—met Rose Chase," she offered hesitantly.

Sam, with his towel halfway around his neck, nodded.

"And you said—or did—something she didn't like?"

"I think you could say that," Sam admitted.

"With this little girl in your office you don't need me," Ortega said. "But I *do* have a few things for you."

"Sit," Sam said as he waved toward the only other chair in the office. "Tell."

"Westbrook has a trust fund from his great-aunt Caroline, but he's been spending out of it like mad. I don't exactly know how big it was originally, but it wasn't enough to buy a Lamborghini for cash, and allow himself to live high on the hog on his salary. Which isn't all that big. His own investments are about as well-off as his clients', which isn't too good. Rumor has it that he's losing money hand over fist. So where he's getting all this spending money from I just don't know. Unless—"

"Unless?"

"Unless he's dipping into his clients' investment portfolios."

"Ah," Sam said as he paced around his desk and sat down again in his super-sized lounge chair. The chair squeaked, and a trickle of water ran down his right pant leg and into his already flooded shoe. "Damn," he muttered. "That's what I get for working undercover!"

He mused for a moment and then said, "I think if you, Mr. Ortega, could follow that line—where is he getting his money from?—it would settle all our problems. Try the radio station. They evidently made some comments on the air on Sunday. Worth checking out.

"And as for you, Veronica, I have a big case in hand so please don't accept any more outside work until I give the word, right?"

After storming out of the Stone Soup, Rosie went home. She snarled at the old tomcat laying on the sidewalk and outgrowled the dog on the corner. Guilt was piling up inside her—guilt for dumping the ice water over Sam Horton, Attorney-at-Law. She tried hard to ignore those feelings. He deserved it, she told herself. And more! Only came to town for one case? Yeah, pull my other leg.

As she came into the house, she slammed the door. It helped somehow. It was childish, but it helped. Millie came out of the kitchen, wiping her hands on her apron.

"Something wrong?" she asked.

"Wrong?" Rose grumbled. "What ever gives you that idea?"

"Because if you frown a little more you'll split your forehead. Calm down, now, girl," Millie said soothingly. "Come in the kitchen and tell Penny and me what's wrong. I'll make you a nice strong cup of tea."

"Penny? She's here?" Rose took several deep breaths and followed Millie into the kitchen. Her housekeeper was evidently teaching Penny the rudiments of cooking. The kitchen floor had an uneven coating of flour and a delicious smell filled the kitchen.

"We're making brownies," Penny said with a big smile. "They should be done in just a few minutes. You can be the first to try them."

"I'm to be sort of an experimental animal?" Rose said, trying to find humor—and missing.

"Naw," Millie drawled, "that be cruelty to animals. We thought we'd start with you and see how it goes." As she said this she poured hot water into a mug with a tea bag already in it and sat it in front of Rose.

"Okay," Penny said after watching Rose swallow some of the tea, "what has my father done to get your goat?"

Rose nearly choked on the tea. "What makes you think I'm angry at your father?"

"It is fairly logical," Millie said. "Only someone for whom you have strong feelings could make you that angry."

"So, what did he do?" Penny was persistent.

Rose stared at both of them. Two smart women, both of whom seem to know more than I do about practically anything in the world! she thought.

"You—don't seem to be mad at me," she said to Penny.

"Mad at you? Me?" Penny grinned at her. "You've got the wrong party. I'm the one who likes you. A lot."

"Even though—your kittens?"

"How could I be mad at you?" the girl said. "You're a nice-looking widow, you own the best radio station in town, and there's every chance I could do a deal with you about my father. A girl would be biting off her nose to spite her face by being mad at you. And besides, you've got the best cook in the village. Now, what's my dad done to spoil things today?"

"He's taken Chad Westbrook as a client," Rose said while trying to fight the tears. "And they both served me with a summons this morning."

"My dad may do a lot of things," Penny said, "but I don't think that even he would do something as stupid as that. I met Mr. Westbrook. He wouldn't even make a good girder for a bridge!"

"I tend to agree with you," Rose returned, "but it was your father's signature on the bottom of the summons, wasn't it?"

"How do you know that?" Penny wondered. "Did Mr. Westbrook say so? Or maybe you just read the identifier under the scrawl my dad uses for a signature.

You don't seem to realize that my dad is working undercover!''

"No," Rose said, distracted by the question, but determined, "it was there as big as life and just as legible. And he was there at the serving. Undercover?''

"Undercover. Or someone is signing his name to papers," his daughter said with conviction. "No one can read his handwriting, much less his signature. Are you sure that Westbrook hired him?''

"Why would Chad lie to me about that?" Rose said, bewildered. "He was overjoyed at getting your father to be his lawyer. It made him think he had a case against me. And your father was right there all the time, grinning away like a Cheshire cat.''

"I don't know that Cheshire cat bit," Penny said, "but I do know about undercover. Had to be. What did my dad say?''

"Say? He didn't say anything. Why would he have to? The papers were clear enough! Neat and to the point.''

"If it was neat my father didn't do it," Penny insisted. "He couldn't—''

Whatever she meant to say didn't come out. Some massive fist banged on the front door. Rose got up and went to answer the knock. "You!''

"Yes, me.''

"Don't you dare come into—''

The rest of the sentence was wasted. Sam Horton took hold of both her upper arms, lifted her off her feet, and set her aside. "My daughter is here," he said. "I want to know just what you're doing with her.''

"Doing with her?" Rose shrilled. "She's in the kitchen. Why don't you ask her what she's doing with us?''

She was talking to the back of his head by that time. The swinging kitchen door closed behind him. Rose shook her head, closed the front door, and followed along behind.

"Penelope!"

"Oh, hi, Dad."

"What the devil are you doing here?"

"Making cookies."

"With—her?"

"With Rose. We're the best of friends, you know."

"You're the—? Since when?"

"Since she's been so nice to me. I've decided to give her one of my kittens. Did you know that?"

"Of *course* I didn't know that. The last time you and I talked you were asking me to sue her for a million dollars. And now everything is peaches and cream. Do you—?"

"Why do you look so wet, Dad?"

"I—because your *best friend* here threw a pitcher of water over me. Ice water."

"You probably deserved it," his daughter said.

Sam Horton took a deep breath. I'll never understand women, he told himself. Young or old, big or small— never. What chance does a man have in this world?

And there this wicked woman stood, not two feet away, looking about as innocent as a newborn lamb. Smiling as if her mouth were stuffed with butter. I ought to do something about that! he told himself. And so he did.

Rose had not been reading his eyes as well as she might. Her ears were tuned to the wonderful music Penny was making. Talking about them being friends for ever, and things like that. As a result, when Horton grabbed her and slammed her up against his steel chest she barely managed an "Oh, my". And by the time she mustered enough anger to fight back there wasn't enough fight left in her to make it worthwhile.

"Attaway," his daughter cheered as he sealed off Rose's mouth.

Rose, unaware, hardly managed a breath as he enveloped her, his warm, tasty lips taking control of her. His strong arms pulled her into a cocoon of comfort.

It hardly seems fair, she said to herself. But her feelings were vague and she really didn't believe all that stuff about fairness and equality among the sexes. No man, she told herself flightily, is ever going to be equal to me. I've got him under control now, and I'll keep kissing him until I live for another hundred years, because women are the dominant sex, and he can't stop me.

But he did.

She looked up at him, surprised. "You stopped?"

"Good for you," Millie said. "Somewhere around here I've got some of that apple cobbler."

"The cookies," Penny yelled. "They're burning!"

"That's your father burning," Millie said, but she moved over to the oven anyway. The brownies were perhaps a shade or two darker than they ought to have been.

"You're a devil," Sam Horton said huskily, concentrating entirely on Rose. He loosened his grip, and both her feet came down flat on the floor.

"You're going to sue me," she suggested.

"Yes. It won't hurt. I'm going to sue you right after I kiss you again."

"Don't you dare!" She licked her lips, hoping he wasn't paying any attention to the conversation. But he was.

It seemed to be several hours later when he let her up for another breath. She shuddered with excitement, her heart going at twice her normal speed.

"Do we have to have all this audience?" he grumbled.

"You'd better believe it," Millie said. "Chaperons, you know. The two of us."

"I wanna see what comes next," Penny commented.

Me too, Rose told herself. Frank was nice, but not as nice as this.

"This is all ever so nice," Millie commented, "but I've got ten thousand cookies all over the place, and a pile of flour on everything, and I can't find the broom."

"We left it in the yard," Penny said.

"And it's been raining like the devil," Sam Horton said. "You won't be able to broom anything—"

"Sweep anything," his daughter corrected him. "Has it stopped raining?"

"Just about," her father reported as he pulled back one of the kitchen curtains.

"Then I could rush up to the other house and bring ours down," Penny said.

"It's pretty dark," Millie said. "Be careful. This is a dangerous street after dark."

"A street like this in a town like this? Impossible," Sam said.

"Impossible hell," Rose said bitterly. They all stared at her.

"She should know," Millie reported.

"My husband, Frank, was run down a year ago three streets away from here, in weather just like this." Rose whirled around to hide her face.

"Hit-and-run," Millie commented. "They never did find out who did it, or how. Killed him dead, it did."

"Please." Rose rubbed her eyes, and then ran out of the room. The three of them heard her shoes rattle on the stairs, then her bedroom door slam behind her as she sought refuge.

The three of them stared at each other for a moment. "Bad luck," Sam murmured.

"You'd better believe it," Millie said. "And it's marked her for all her life," she added, sighing. "I just had the feeling that she'd been working her way out of it these past few weeks, but now—"

Silence.

"But we still need the broom," Penny said. "I'll go get it."

"Carefully," her father cautioned. "Stay on the sidewalk all the way. If anyone comes near you, blow the siren on your wheelchair."

"Aw, Dad. Come on, now. I've lived a lot of years in Boston. This place couldn't compare."

The two adults looked at each other and shrugged. "All right," Sam said reluctantly. "Don't dillydally."

Penny was out the front door before any more objections could be raised. "I hate to limit her," Sam said. "She needs to learn independence."

"And she's a very dependable girl," Millie agreed. "Have some of this apple cobbler. It's the best ever."

From upstairs they could hear the muffled sobs.

CHAPTER SIX

"GOOD tasting—what did you call it?" Sam Horton dipped his fork into his second helping and grinned. Rose, who had finally dried her tears and returned downstairs, cut him another piece and had it ready for third helpings.

"Cobbler. Apple cobbler. You've never heard of it before?" Millie looked across the table in surprise.

"Can't say as I have," Horton said. "But then, my mother was never much of a cook. Seems to me that she needed a guide dog to find the kitchen, to be truthful about it."

"Well, not every woman turns out to be a good cook," Millie offered. "Where in the world do you come from, son?"

"The middle west," he told her. "Near Sandusky, Ohio."

"Oh, well, I suppose your mother had some other fine traits. A hobby, a business—something like that?"

"Not so's I can remember," Sam said, shaking his head. "I think she considered that there was enough money in the family and she didn't need to do *anything*." Both the women in the kitchen with him laughed.

"Not true?" he asked.

"Not true," Millie said.

"Rose can cook?"

"Don't embarrass me," Rose said. "Yes, Rose can cook. Not as well as Millie, of course, but good enough."

"But if you had a million dollars to your name you wouldn't be cooking, Rose, would you?"

"Hah," Millie chuckled. "Rose has a good deal more than a million in her bank account. And she made the apple cobbler that you're smackin' your lips over. Before she inherited that idiot radio station she used to do most all the cooking in this house. Make some man a fine wife, Rose—"

"Millie!"

"Well, it's true, Rose Mary."

"Not something to boast about," Rose muttered. "More coffee, Mr. Horton?"

"Believe I will, if it's for offer."

"Oh, it's for offer," Rose murmured. And why is it that he appears so—easy to get along with tonight, I wonder? she thought. And does he know how damnably attractive it makes him? I wish I could turn back the clock a few weeks and meet Sam Horton all over again!

There was a rattle at the east windows.

"More rain," Millie announced. "I hope Penny doesn't get soaked on the way back."

"Don't worry about her," Sam Horton said. "She's Miss Practical Pig. Able to look after herself under any circumstances. And besides, it's only a block away."

"Yes," Rose said, "and she's only twelve years old. That's not a heck of a lot of years, and that's one of the busiest streets in—"

Tires whined as a car went by in the rain. And then another set of tires, moving at high speed, slipping and sliding and screeching on the road.

"Like that," Rose said. Her hands locked on the sides of her chair, her fingers turning rigidly white. There was a sound of brakes from out of the darkness, a skidding of tires, and a dull thud, followed by a metallic crash.

Sam Horton upset the table as he pushed away from it. "Penny!" he yelled. As the words echoed he was at the front door.

Millie was close behind him, her movements stifled by age and arthritis, but still moving.

Rose struggled to her feet and then seemed to freeze in position, unable to move one way or another, locked in a paralysis of fear. Her hands twisted against each other in front of her, but no matter how she commanded herself nothing but her fingers moved. Outside a motor roared as an automobile backed away a few feet, paused, and raced off into the darkness.

Millie rushed back into the house, took one look at Rose and then grabbed her by both shoulders and shook her hard.

"Call 911," she yelled. "It's no time to lock yourself up. Rose! No time to panic!"

"I—what?" Rose wailed. "What?"

"It's Penny," Millie shouted at her. "Don't lock up on yourself at a time like this. Call the emergency number." Another hard shake.

"Penny?" Rose managed a deep breath. "Yes."

She moved over to the corner table where the telephone rested and picked up the instrument. "I—forgot the number."

"911," Millie yelled at her. "911." The housekeeper snatched up her emergency nurse's bag from the kitchen closet and dashed back out the door.

Rose stood by the telephone table, the instrument in her hand; her whole body shook, bumping the handset against her jaw. Finally she bit her lip, felt the sting of it all, and dialed the right number. "There's been an accident," she screamed, and managed to give the address.

Millie slapped her bag down on the sidewalk. "Don't try to move her," she ordered. "Lord knows what's broken. Any movement might do terrible damage."

Sam Horton, who was just about to make the try, drew back. The heavy wheelchair was lying on its side on the inner edge of the sidewalk, the upper main wheel spinning slowly. Penny was trapped inside the chair, caught by the shattered aluminum arm, her eyes closed.

"Don't try to move her," Millie repeated. "You can't tell what's happened to her. See if you can cover her from the rain!"

Sam dashed for the house at high speed and snatched a pair of raincoats from the coat rack by the front door and then reversed his field. Rose was standing at the kitchen door, frozen, trembling.

"Did you get the emergency service?" he asked. She nodded, and took a step in his direction. She needed comforting, he knew. Her face was ash-pale with shock, but he knew that she had to come second. She reached one hand in his direction. He snatched at it and kissed it, and then ran for the door. As the screen door slammed behind him two tiny tears formed and ran down Rose's cheek.

Millie was down on her hands and knees, doing her best to make Penny comfortable. Sam skidded down beside her and passed the two raincoats over to the more experienced hands. Millie arranged a sort of tent to cover the little girl, and then dug out her stethoscope to check Penny's vital signs. In the distance, over on Bridge Street, they could hear the roar of the siren on the rescue truck as it zoomed out of its shelter only a couple of blocks away.

"Some problem with her left leg," Millie told him. "Probably a green stick fracture. And perhaps something with her right hip. Nothing else that I can see. They'll be here in a minute."

And they were; the rescue ambulance arrived, all lights and sirens, shepherded by the fire pumper truck, running like a football blocking back, sweeping traffic off the roads in all directions. By guess, they were at the scene in less than five minutes. Some distance behind them, having come all the way from Dartmouth Center, a lone police car wheeled down the curving narrow road and thundered over the bridge.

In the kaleidoscope of action and reaction there seemed to be no place for a lawyer. Sam Horton backed off and watched. Two of the rescue personnel lifted the Jaws of Life, a massive pair of metal cutters, out of their truck and with infinite skill cut through the narrow aluminum arm that held Penny trapped in her chair. Moments later they had the girl out of the wreckage and strapped onto a transport-board.

The police car pulled up beside the ambulance, and its driver came over to Sam. "Tell me what happened."

"All my damn fault," Horton said. "I sent my daughter up to the corner house on a stupid errand. It seemed so simple. Then some crazy driver came rushing up the street, hit her wheelchair, and knocked her into the bushes. Hit-and-run. If I ever find him I'll kill the bastard!"

"Easy," the big policeman said. "Take it easy. This is the best rescue squad in Southern Massachusetts. Now, did you *see* what happened?"

"Nothing," Sam said bitterly. "I didn't see a thing. God! I was sitting in that house over there, all happy and warm, eating apple cobbler. All I heard was the sound. I could kill the—"

"Yeah, I know," the policeman sympathized. "And if we ever catch him they'll probably give him a year in the county jail and a stern warning! Who the hell is this zombie coming up the sidewalk?"

Sam Horton wiped the rain and tears out of his eyes. Coming down the sidewalk, walking mechanically, one slow step at a time, was Rose Chase.

"Oh, my God," Sam said as he stumbled in Rose's direction. She stopped as he came up to her and enveloped her in both arms. At least, he told himself, here's one I can comfort. "Rose?"

She walked into his chest, rigid as a steel rod, unbending, not weakening. "Penny's dead?" she asked. "Like Frank, Penny's dead?"

"Not likely," Sam said. The ambulance, loaded, backed around.

"I'm going with the ambulance," Millie said. "To Saint Luke's in New Bedford. Look after Rose Mary. She needs a lot of help."

"Not dead?" Rose queried.

"Not dead, love."

And with that all the strength, all the vitality fled from Rose's tiny body. She collapsed against him and sobbed her heart out. Sam, not an inch away from her, folded her up and joined her with his own tears.

"Put her in my car," the policeman ordered. "I've got to go to the hospital anyway, and she looks as badly off as the child in the wheelchair."

"When will we know something?" Rose whispered. They were seated together in the waiting lounge just outside the emergency room at St. Luke's Hospital. It was almost midnight, but the corridors were still thronged. Solemn, white-clothed figures moved in all directions, with not a smile to be seen.

"Not long," Sam returned. "Another hour, perhaps. Maybe two."

"I feel like a fool," Rose told him. "I—didn't expect to freeze like I did. Just when she needed me I wasn't there. It— "

He cupped her hand inside his massive grip. "You've nothing to apologize for Rose. Millie explained it all to me."

"Everything?"

"Everything. That was the way your husband died, wasn't it?"

"Yes." She leaned closer to him and nuzzled his wet shoulder. "Yes. The same way, three streets over, and almost the same time. But he was—gone before I got to his side."

"Tell me about him."

"About Frank?" He put his arm around her and gently tugged her head down onto his shoulder. "Frank and I, we grew up together. His family lived in that empty house next to yours. We went to school together, all the way from kindergarten to high school. And then we went off to college, and after that he volunteered for the Army and went off to Somalia for four years."

"And when he came back you married?"

"Not exactly," Rose said. "Frank came back—in a wheelchair. He lost both his legs to a land mine."

"So much like Penny," Sam murmured.

"He needed someone to take care of him. So we married. It was the only thing to do, wasn't it?" It was a plaintive question, as if she wanted assurance that what she had done was right.

He patted her head gently. Of course, he thought. It was the only thing to do. But not a word about love, dear little Rose. Duty, but not love. "I can't judge," he said. "But it probably was the only worthwhile thing to do."

"You *do* understand, Sam, don't you?" One of her tiny, cold hands came up and caressed his face. And she sighed. "His mother never *did* understand. But she said she couldn't take care of him. She had a fear of sickness and sick people." The hand came back to his face. "I'll bet you have to shave twice a day, don't you?"

"Most of the time," he admitted. "I often thought I ought to grow a beard, but then, I just never got around to it."

"I'm glad."

"Where is Frank's mother now?"

"Who knows?" She shrugged. "She packed up one night and disappeared. Nobody's ever heard of her since. That was the last straw. Frank and I married the next day. Wasn't that an awful thing to do?"

"Awful." But I'm not sure whether I mean his mother's flight or your marriage, he told himself. And you're glad that I never grew a beard? You're not forever mad at me, are you?

She interrupted his thoughts. "Where's Millie?"

"She came in the ambulance with Penny. I thought I'd do better staying with you. And after we caught up here at the hospital I sent her home. She's probably a fine nurse, but not the youngest one in the world. She looked terribly tired and was glad to go. And you ought to go home as well."

She struggled to sit up. "No. Not me. Penny is my— friend. I *have* to stay here. She might need me."

"You're not too well yourself, girl. You know when we arrived in the emergency room the doctor treated you for shock?"

"But he—gave me something and then said I should rest. That's what I'm doing. Resting." Rose settled back in her chair and leaned over onto his shoulder again.

"You need bed rest, Rose."

She giggled and tucked her hand under his arm. "Is that an offer, Mr. Horton?"

"That's—"

The doctor came in at that moment and threw all Sam's ideas out the window.

"Dr. Calton," he announced. "You're the Hortons?"

"Yes?"

"Your daughter is a very lucky girl. Very lucky."

"I'm glad to hear you say that," Sam Horton said doubtfully. He came to his feet and paced up and down the narrow room. Rose slipped off his shoulder and caught herself just in time. He turned around to the doctor. "In what way is she lucky?"

"I wouldn't say she doesn't have problems. But they are things that can be cured. Her left hip is damaged, her leg is broken, and she has a concussion. We've done what's necessary—for the moment—to her leg, cleaned up the scratches on her head, and put her to bed. She's in Recovery now. Later we'll move her into the children's ward. She'll probably sleep for twenty-four hours or so."

"So I can see her?"

"Well . . ." The doctor stroked his chin and dropped into the chair that Sam Horton had vacated. In the better light the strain lines on his face were visible.

"See her, yes. But I doubt if she'll be able to see you—or talk to you. Not for a day or so."

"And then?"

"And then we'll know better, won't we? Why don't you and her mother go down there?"

"But I'm not her mother," Rose said. "I wish—"

"My mistake," Dr. Calton said. "I guess I've been up too late. But the little girl keeps mumbling that same litany over and over."

"Mumbling?"

"Yes. Every now and again she sports a little smile and says 'Mama Rose'. I just drew the wrong conclusion. I've got to get back to work. Good luck to you both."

Sam Horton watched as the doctor plunged through the double doors at considerable speed, and then turned to Rose.

"So what do you think of that?" he asked gently. "You wish—what?"

"I—it's none of your business," Rose answered as she turned her head away from him.

"No more running away, Rose." His one hand on her shoulder turned her back in his direction. "You wish what?"

"Damn you! I wish I *were* her mother!"

"It can be arranged," he said jauntily. "But you'd have to take me in the bargain."

"That's rather a lot of bargain," she said glumly. "You're not exactly the prize at the fair, you know."

"There are always those little problems, Rose."

She took a quick peek at him, then brought her attention back to the floor. Those deep brown eyes had almost caught her. And maybe that's what I want, she told herself. To be caught like flypaper; trapped for life?

Trapped? What is love, anyway? Is it this hot passion that runs through me every time I look at him? So far only anger helps me fight him off. And the honest truth is I don't think I want to be angry with him all the time.

What is it, then, this love? Here I am, a widow at twenty-seven, and I don't know what love is. But then I never was in love with Frank. I was comfortable with him; we knew each other inside out. I sympathized with him. But never love.

But one thing's for sure. I'd never be *comfortable* with Sam. He sets me on fire.

"So why don't we go over to the recovery room?" he suggested. The words startled Rose, still deep in her reverie.

"Good idea," she mumbled.

A passing technician with a cart full of blood samples was going that way, and cheerfully guided them. "I don't think they'll let you in," she advised, "but at least you can look through the window."

"There!" Rose exclaimed. "Right by the side window. Look, she's smiling!"

"She's fast asleep," Sam retorted. "Well, maybe she *is* smiling. Mama Rose, do you suppose that's what she's dreaming about?"

"Don't push your luck," Rose snapped.

"Funny thing... I've dreamed that same thing more than once," he countered.

A shiver ran up Rose's spine. *He* dreamed? How could that be? She couldn't understand, so she asked.

"Why not, little Rose? You're the right age, the right size, a beauty if ever there was one. Full of grit and determination. Do you have any doubts that Penny loves you?"

"I—no, I guess I—"

"So why should you have any doubts that *I* love you too?"

"But *that's* different," Rose said.

"Different how?" He turned her around to face him.

"Don't tease me, Sam," she begged.

"I'm not teasing. You've never had a more sincere man at your feet, Rose."

"I don't *want* a man at my feet," she snapped. "I want a man who—"

"Who will be the man of the house," he retorted. "And that I am and will be. Want proof?"

"Sam—not here. Everyone is watching!"

"Good for them. They'll learn a little something."

That was the end of the conversation. He gathered her up, bag and baggage. Swept her off her feet, leaving her toes six inches off the floor. For a moment her tiny hands beat at his shoulders, and then they quietly wound themselves around his neck in triumphant surrender.

I ought to tell him I love him, she thought, and she opened her mouth to do just that, but too late. He bent his head to her. His lips sealed hers warmly, gently, and

Rose gave up the effort. A moment or two of that comfort, and then there was a lightning flash that stunned her.

Rose had kissed more than one man or boy in her lifetime. She was a closed-eye kisser. But this lightning strike from Sam Horton so startled her that her eyes flew open wider than she had thought possible.

She gasped, vainly seeking air. He released her from bondage and grinned. She inhaled and did her best to glare at him.

"Wise guy," she muttered, and squirmed closer to mount her own attack.

Sam Horton had also kissed his share of females, but he was certainly not accustomed to ferocious feline female responses. He hung in there for dear life, not quite controlling this woman, but at least not dropping her.

"Ooh, look at that," said the woman who had joined them at the window.

"Horton? Are you Horton?" asked the heavy male voice. Sam opened one eye. The policeman had joined the admiring little crowd. Sam slowly opened both eyes, and gently lowered Rose so her feet could touch the floor. She half stumbled; he held her close and looked over her head at the cop.

"There's always one spoilsport in every crowd," that worthy said. "If you're Horton, just nod your head. I have a few questions to ask."

Hospital lounges, especially late at night, were not always the most pleasant places in the world. Oh, they were clean, usually neat, and occasionally decorated with a mural or two. St. Luke's, being the principal hospital in the town called the Whaling City, was over-decorated with paintings of old whaling ships and hunts at sea. It was all old hat to Rose, who had been born and bred in southeastern New England. She settled down on a hard divan next to Sam, and was grateful when his arm came over her shoulder and pulled her close.

But to Sam it was all new. It took him more than a few minutes to get adjusted. Not just to the paintings, but to the warm softness of Rosie Chase, cuddled up against him.

"Tell me everything you can about the accident," the policeman said. Sam waited patiently for the officer to whip out his notebook. No such thing happened.

"Go ahead," the cop urged.

"You don't write things down?"

"This modern age," the officer said, chuckling. He reached into his uniform pocket and pulled out a little tape recorder. "You were saying?"

Sam shook his head and grinned. "Everything changes," he commented. "Well, I don't know all that much. I came out of the house immediately I heard the crash. My daughter's wheelchair was on its side in the bushes. Evidently this driver actually came up onto the sidewalk and hit her."

"What kind of a car?"

"One of those little two-seater sports cars. I couldn't tell what color it was. Those streetlights are yellow, you know. It was light green, perhaps. Or maybe blue." Rose squirmed against him to become better settled. He stopped, and freed one hand to stroke her soft hair.

"I wasn't paying all that much attention to the car. I was going my hardest to get to my daughter." He coughed and cleared his throat. "I don't know who was a bigger fool than me, letting her go out like that, but she was always so insistent on being independent. What my daughter needs—"

"Is a mother," Rose interjected. The pair of them stared at each other, exchanging a silent message. The policeman scratched the side of his head and waited patiently.

Sam gave Rose another squeeze. "Is a mother," he confirmed.

"Did you see who was driving?"

"Not really. It was a man, but I couldn't make out any sort of description. The car was one of those racing things. He was sitting very low in the seat but the windows were semi-opaque. He was—wearing a cap of some sort. He knew he hit her. The front of his car was up on the sidewalk. He put his lights out just as I came out of the house. And then he backed up and went up the street at full speed. Without any lights. I couldn't see his license plates, but they looked to be Massachusetts plates. And that's about it."

Rose caught up the hand that rested on her shoulder and squeezed it hard for comfort. Well, not all that hard, but the best she could do. Her mind was wandering. They had given her something to calm her down, and now her world was placid.

"Is there any chance you'll catch him?" Sam asked.

The officer snapped off his recorder and put it back into his pocket. "There's a fair chance," he said. "He scraped off a good bit of the paint from his front end. According to our lab the car was light blue. We'll keep looking. Hit-and-run drivers don't often get away from us."

"Hah!" Rose snorted. The officer looked questioningly at her.

"Her husband," Sam explained. "He was killed on that same stretch of road by a hit-and-run driver."

"I know," the officer said. "Frank Hamilton, wasn't it? We haven't forgotten; we haven't given up."

Rose gave a big sigh, but said nothing. The policeman nodded to them both, got up and started for the door.

He stopped by the painting of the whaling ship. "My great-grandfather sailed on a ship like that," he said.

He started down the hall, whistling. A passing nurse hushed him.

"*My* great-grandfather owned that ship," Rose boasted as she snuggled even closer to the big man at her side. "And was the captain."

"*My* great-grandfather was the best hog slaughterer in the middle west," Sam Horton said proudly. "Wanna wrestle?"

Penny Horton woke up at six o'clock the next evening, just as the nurses brought in a gurney to take her to the children's ward. "What happened?" the little girl asked. "I'm so thirsty. Mama?"

Rose reached over and patted her hand. "Right here," she said. The recovery-room nurse appeared with a glass of water and a straw. Rose took it and held it to Penny's parched lips.

"Just a sip," she instructed. "You were in an accident, my love. A man ran into you."

"Poor man." Penny tried to shake her head, but there was too much pain.

"Poor man? Why do you say that?"

"'Cos my dad'll kill him. Do you mean that?"

"Do I mean what?"

"'My love'. You said 'my love'. Do you mean that?"

"Of course I mean that," Rose said softly. "For ever and ever."

"But there's my dad—and my real mother," Penny said hesitantly.

"Not to worry," Rose said with a superior expression on her face. "I'm going to be your real mother. Your dad and I are going to get married."

"And does my dad know that?"

"He'll do what he's told," Rose said, and laughed. "At least I think he will. We're going to be married next Tuesday."

"Wheee!" the girl shouted, and then she groaned as her injured head felt the shock. "It's not easy to sit up. All you have to do is be firm with him." The aides were wheeling the gurney down the hall and into the elevator. Penny held on with both hands, until Rose rescued one of those hands and walked beside her.

"Him who?" Rose asked.

"With my dad, of course. I'll help you. I know all the tricks in the book."

"I think perhaps you're overestimating," Rose said. "Being a daughter and being a wife are two different things. Hold steady now. Here's your new bed."

"Oh, I know all about wives," Penny said. "Don't worry about it. I'll coach you. Just remember, be firm."

"Yeah," said the male voice behind them. "Be firm! Who are we being firm with?"

"Hi, Daddy."

"Hi, little girl. Who are we being firm with?"

"Not we. Rose."

"Ah. Rose." His rough voice turned into silky softness. "And who should my Rose be firm with?"

"Millie," Rose said quickly. It was the only name she could think of at the moment, and like any religious coward Rose Chase had no intention of sticking her neck out. "Millie," she repeated. "I don't like—er—oatmeal for breakfast, and she is not to make that any more. Not if I'm firm. Right?"

"Yes," Sam Horton murmured. "Be as firm as you please, but remember, I'm the king of the hill in this family."

Penny looked up at her father, and then over at Rose. "This is where it starts, Rose," she whispered. "Be firm."

Rose swallowed a time or two. Things were not likely to be as easy as she had thought.

"Rose?" Sam asked.

"Yes," she answered. "Be firm. Yes, sir."

She might have said something else, but at that moment an elderly man, trailed by half a dozen nurses, interns and administrators, came down the corridor.

Sam stepped forward and offered a large grin and a very small bow. "Rose," he said, "I want you to meet Dr. Orlop, from Boston Children's Hospital and the Harvard Medical School. He's been Penny's specialist ever since we all moved to New England. Doctor, my fiancée, Rose Chase."

The elderly doctor, his white Vandyke beard glittering in the bright light of the wards, brushed aside all the introductions.

"Mr. Horton," he said, his voice gravelly with age. "I have looked again at your daughter's records, especially those from the last few weeks. I think now it may be possible, with one operation, to correct the malalignment of her leg and her hip. But it will, as my students say, cost you a bundle!"

"You mean—*cure*?"

"I mean cure. There is a good possibility."

"I think I can borrow the money," Sam said. "My father is president of the Green Mountain Bank. I think he'd be more than willing to arrange a loan in aid of his only granddaughter."

Rose Chase, whose memory of things financial was not to be topped by anyone in the banking business, tugged at Sam's sleeve. "Tell him to go ahead, Sam," she said firmly. "Start now."

"But I have to get a loan first," Sam interjected.

"You've got it," Rose said. "I own eighty percent of the stock in the Green Mountain Bank."

Rose didn't quite know what to expect, but certainly it wasn't what happened. Her fiancé took her by the arm and towed her a few steps away from the crowd.

"Don't *do* that," he whispered urgently. "I told you, I'm the boss in this family. You and I are equal, but not very! I'll get the money. Got it?"

Rose was a woman who learned quickly. If he wanted to believe he was in charge of the world, why should *she* disabuse him? "Yes," she said solemnly. "Yes, sir."

"Go right ahead, Doctor," Sam called. "I'll get the money."

Yes, sir, Rose told herself. Call the bank tomorrow morning and approve the loan!

CHAPTER SEVEN

ROSE managed to get home at about two in the afternoon. Millie, who had spent the midnight hours at Penny's bedside, was just getting up. Both of them were worn out from their attendance at the sickbed of the little girl.

"Well, it'll be easier from now on," Rose announced. "I managed to wiggle around the objections and hire three nurses to—what do they call that?"

"Special," Millie filled in. "What in the world took so long? There are dozens of nurses around these parts eager to have an easy special job."

"Millie, don't you say a word about this. I'm going to marry that man no matter what he thinks. Or what I have to do to make it happen. I'll kiss his foot every day—before the wedding, that is."

Millie smiled at her. "I'd have to be deaf, dumb and blind not to see what's going on," she said. "Any time soon?"

"Just as soon as I can. But there's a problem."

"There's always a problem, love. You had one with Frank, you'll remember."

"Yes. But I knew what that problem was, Millie, and the solution was simple."

"And this one you don't know?"

"This one—I'm not sure. I married Frank because it seemed to be my duty. But with Sam..."

"Duty just as well, isn't it? Someone to look after Penny?"

"Or my money, I thought. So I asked him."

116

"And he said?"

"He said he didn't give a damn about my money, because he had enough of his own to take care of Penny—and me as well."

"So that leaves?"

Rose shuddered. "I'm scared to admit the truth. He said he wanted to marry me for my pure sweet body!"

"Now that," Millie said, chuckling, "sounds like a lot of fun!"

"Millie!"

"Well, it's true. Admit it."

"Yes," Rose said, shuffling around in her chair nervously. "But I've never heard it put so—bluntly. And I don't know how to handle it."

"Nevertheless you're going to marry him?"

"Of course I am. I'd be a fool if I didn't. Wouldn't I?"

"I don't give marital advice on Fridays," Millie said. "But what does that have to do with hiring three specials to be with Penny?"

"It's all part of the package," Rose said, embarrassed. "He's the boss, he says. He says I can put my money away in my piggy bank, because he's going to make all the final decisions, and pay all the bills."

"So what did you do?"

Rose shrugged. "What could I do but agree? Frank used to leave everything to me. Sam is that 'horse of a different color'. And—"

"And Rose Mary Chase is too accustomed to doing her own thing. Right?"

"Don't tease me, Millie. I *might* give a little now and then, but he can't expect me just to toe the line day and night, snap to—like that."

"Yes, I can see that," Millie said. "I don't expect you'll have any difficulty toeing the line at night, but I *would* offer you a suggestion for daytime use."

"What suggestion?"

"Just in case things don't go your way, why don't you buy yourself an extra pair of shoes, just in case there's a *lot* of 'snap to' work in your family and heel-clicking? That kind of life is hard on shoe heels." And with that Millie O'Doul walked back up the stairs, laughing so hard that there were tears in her eyes!

"Oh, you," Rose Chase muttered as she reached for the telephone. "So I *won't* tell you how I sweet-talked him into hiring three nurses. So there!"

Mr. Albert Finnerty was the senior trust officer at the Harbor Bank in New Bedford. Had been, for a fact, for thirty-five years or more. He had known Rose for most of her life; she remembered particularly the lollypop he had given her on her fifth birthday, the day her mother brought her in to introduce her, and to open her first trust account. Lollypops, in those long-ago days, had been considerable bribes for good behavior, and Rose had never forgotten.

Albert Finnerty had a voice like a foghorn. "Rose Mary," he roared into the telephone, "it's been a long time since I've heard from you. About time for you to come in to review your accounts."

"Why would I do that, Uncle Albert?" she asked. "I've got you to keep me safe."

"Because it's the account that lies dormant that gets into trouble, my dear. Now, what can I do for you?"

"I want to use your influence, please. With the Green Mountain Bank."

"Green Mountain. Yes, I know one or two people up there. What's the trouble?"

"There's a wonderful little girl down here in Padanaram who needs a very expensive operation, and her father is—er—"

"Broke? Pigheaded?"

"Yes, perhaps one of each of those. He's going to the Green Mountain Bank for a loan to pay for the operation, but he doesn't want anyone to help him. When I told him I owned a piece of the bank he blew his stack. He's just starting out as a lawyer and I thought, because I have all those bonds in the Green Mountain, that a word from me—us—you—might do something to help him get the loan."

All this was said at triple speed, leaving Rose completely out of breath.

There was a massive clearing of throat from the other end. "Well," her trustee said. "I'm sure if I mention your name and run down some of your income holdings they'd be glad to comply. Or we could consolidate those Union Pacific bonds I've been coaxing you about for the past five years. We could convert them, and perhaps deposit a couple of million in the Green Mountain. That would certainly get their attention."

"I—don't understand," Rose said, confused. "I've got all those Green Mountain bonds already, and—"

"Rose Mary," Finnerty said slowly. "I do believe your mind is slipping. You don't remember that two months ago you authorized your Padanaram broker to sell off the Green Mountain bonds?"

"I—what?"

"Your broker. That big fellow. Westriver?"

"Westbrook," Rose murmured.

"Yes, that's the man. Said you wanted to make a massive investment in land in the Padanaram area. Which, by the way, is one fine thing to do, what with land values shooting up the way they are."

"So you cashed the Green Mountain bonds?"

"And gave him a cashier's check for the whole. How's the investment going, Rose? I've only another month or so until retirement, and this fellow appears to be a bright young man. The sort who could take over all of your portfolio and do you some good. Youth is where it's at, Rose Mary."

"I'm sure you're right," Rose said quietly as her mind turned over at a phenomenal rate. Cashier's check? Bright young man? Take over *all* her assets? What in the world was Chad Westbrook up to? All this on top of his civil suit? Right after I marry Sam Horton I believe I should strangle Chad in his own necktie. I could claim temporary insanity. I certainly never authorized him to make any transactions without my prior approval, she thought.

"Well, until you make up your mind, Rose, I'll go ahead and contact the Green Mountain people. Keep me posted on your land investment. I may come across something along that line which might help. Anything else new, love?"

"Uncle Al—I'm going to get married again."

"Well, good for you, my dear. He's a lucky fellow. It wouldn't be young Westbrook, by any chance?"

"I don't think so. I mean—no, it certainly won't be Chad Westbrook."

"So whoever he is I congratulate him. Come see me soon."

"Yes, sir," she said softly, musingly, as her busy mind pursued the new information. A cashier's check, no less. There was no way of stopping action on a cashier's check. She wheeled around in her chair and pulled the cover off her hardly used computer. It was an old personal computer, but still functional, and some years ago, for the fun of it, she had entered all her holdings on a pair of disks in that computer. She inserted the proper disks, pushed a couple of buttons, the screen lit up and the Green Mountain account answered her summons. Four years old, the entry was. Four hundred and fifty one thousand dollars. Not counting all the accrued interest.

Millie clattered down the stairs dressed for an evening of entertainment at the church bingo games, and looked surprised. "Seems like forever since you had that thing turned on," the housekeeper said. "Some trouble?"

Rose flipped the "off" switch on the computer terminal and struggled to her feet. "Millie, you know I've always thought I was too smart to be tricked?"

"Of course. Your father was the same. So?"

"Millie, I was wrong. I'm not that smart. I think I've been robbed."

Sam Horton came by in his wagon at four o'clock, parked by the side of the road, and came in without knocking. "Visiting hours start at six-thirty," he said. "Would you like to come along?"

"I would indeed," Rose responded. He looked rumpled, his suit no longer neat, his tie awry, his cheeks almost sunken. "When did you last eat a decent meal?"

"I don't believe I can remember that far back," Sam said. Millie had set one place at the kitchen table before she went off. Rose carried the steaming tureen of beef stew to the table. His eyes followed her every step of the way.

"We've got enough for three," Rose offered. "Three and a half. What have you done with the cats?"

"That's the easy part," he said. Up until that moment his face had been solemn, his brown eyes darkened by fatigue. Now suddenly he came to life, smiling. "I had some cat food in the closet. I was almost tempted to try it myself, but—"

"But it was too much for you?" Rose asked.

He was a big, well-developed man, but for the veriest second or two he blushed. "No, not that," he said, shaking his head. "I knew for a fact that if I came by early enough you'd feed me."

"Men!" Rose snatched another plate from the closet and set another place at the table, keeping her back to him so that he couldn't see her smile.

"Did they teach that at law school?" she asked mischievously.

"Yes, indeed. Survival 101. I got an A plus. The highest mark of my entire student career."

"Sit," she commanded. It did her a world of good to have him under her thumb, even for such a little time.

"Millie isn't eating with us?"

"No. Tonight is bingo night, and she gets a nervous stomach before the games start. Sit."

But he hadn't forgotten. Not even for the price of a good hot meal. He grinned a slow grin at her, then casually pursued her around the table, until she backed into the serving side table.

"I give the orders, babe," he said in that soft, deep, tantalizing voice.

"After we're married," Rose asserted indignantly. "I'm my own woman until after the 'I do' part of the ceremony."

He took another step in her direction and his hands fell on her shoulders. "Technically correct," he murmured.

She shivered in anticipation. "That's not fair," she protested weakly.

"Indeed? You've never heard about all's fair in love and war?"

It's too late to run, Rose told herself, and there's no place to run to, and besides, what he's threatening might be—

And it was. Soft, warm lips covered her own. Comforting, gradually growing stronger. Demanding. She opened her mouth to protest and lost the whole ball game. His questing tongue came through her barriers and searched out every tender space within. One of his hands came off her shoulders to pull her closer within his trap. The other dropped lower, caressing her just at her hip line.

And that's not fair either, Rose told herself as she squirmed to get closer. Fire ran up and down her spine, shattering her nerve control. Some woman in the room was moaning. Rose closed her ears, only to transfer all those sensations to her eyes. The feeling was too strong; she closed her eyes, still fighting.

"Who's the boss?" he whispered in her ear.

"After the 'I do'," she returned in a wobbly voice.

"Say 'I do', Rose."

She fought on for perhaps another two seconds, and then, with a gusty sigh, said, "I do," as all her muscles and her mind relaxed.

His lips came back down on her, sealing her mouth. Her head dissolved; there seemed to be fourth of July rockets shooting off. Next he'll carry me upstairs, and then the dinner will get cold, Rose told herself, but it's been a long time since I sampled the flesh, and he—

And he released the pressure on her lips, added a little hug at hip and shoulder, and gradually released her. "Now," he said, "we'll eat."

Totally confused, Rose put both hands behind her back and twisted her fingers around each other nervously. "You don't want to go upstairs?"

"Oh, I want to, but that's the chocolate cake, my dear. And that we'll save until right after the wedding. Only you'd better not delay in running down the stairs of the church!"

"Good God, I love you." She hurled herself at him, using the full length of her arms to embrace him, but not quite able to get them completely around him.

"Thank God for that," he said, sighing with relief. "For the past couple of days I had the feeling you thought I wanted you just to look after Penny."

"Penny? Who's Penny?" she teased.

He swept her up in his arms and set her down not too gently on one of the kitchen chairs. "Eat," he commanded. "Some day soon you'll need your strength."

So she ate daintily, keeping one eye on him and his spoon. No doubt about it, he was a trencherman of great renown. And when he was finished he tilted his plate to be sure he got all the goodness out of it.

"Good stuff," he pronounced as he put his utensil down. "Millie can sure cook up a storm. Do we get to keep her after the wedding?"

"For your information, *Mr.* Horton, I made that stew all by myself."

"Okay, okay," he said as he faked a ducking away from her. "So you can cook stew. Who could ask for better?"

"I am also," she said in a very superior tone, "known as an expert with liver and onions. Very healthy, that."

"Not in *my* house," he said. "I don't eat the stuff, my daughter won't eat the stuff— C'mon, lady, we've a couple of hours to spare, the sun is bright, the birds are singing. Let's take a ride to—"

"To where?"

"Round Hill. You do know where that is, don't you?"

"Yes. Do you?"

"Hey, none of that smart stuff, lady. No, I don't know where it is, but I read a pamphlet over at the hospital which claimed it was the finest sight in the area."

"I know that pamphlet," she told him. "It was written some time ago."

"Be exact. When?"

"How about like 1936?"

"That is a time ago," he agreed. "There's been some changes since?"

"Well, for one thing, the old Colonel is dead. I don't think it would be worth your while to drive out that far. It's at the tip of Round Hill Point, you know."

"I have something on my mind, love. So naturally we'll go. Us Horton men aren't very often wrong. You need to memorize that."

"Oh? Another one of those things I have to submit to after I do the 'I do' bit?"

"You've got it, love. Let's be with it."

They made a brief stop at his house to check up on the two kittens and their mother, and then, sitting high in the front seat of the wagon, Rose gave directions. "You know, of course, I could drive it myself and save us a lot of time, Sam."

"Not a chance," he said. "I drive, you enjoy. Do you have a license?"

"Of course I do. Since I was sixteen. Turn right on Bridge Street and cross the bridge."

"And with all that money you don't have a car?"

"I have two of them. I keep them in storage up in New Bedford."

"You own two cars and have to ride around in a taxi? Millie told me you *never* drive. How come?"

"I did once, some years ago, but since Frank—I haven't been behind the wheel since the day of his funeral."

"There are a lot of things you haven't been doing, aren't there, Rosie? We'll have to do something about all of them. It's time you were back on the average track."

"I'm not a mental cripple," Rose snapped. "I can drive if I want to, and I don't want you to think you're some sort of Svengali, Mr. Horton. Turn left ahead there, on Smith Neck Road. And don't call me Rosie!"

"Oh, wow. We're in some sort of a snit, aren't we?"

"No, *I am not*! I'm just a typical American girl, who doesn't want to be dictated to by some huge, arrogant male!"

"Wedding's off, Rose?"

"I'm not that big a fool. Look over there to the left."

"Houses. That's all I see—houses."

"That's the village of Nonquit," she told him. "And see that house on the outskirts? That's Chad Westbrook's place." The car slowed as he lifted his foot from the gas pedal.

"Right there, huh? Why does it look so big?"

"Right there. The house is not really all that big. Chad has a thing about cars. I'm not sure, but I think about half of that building is really a three- or four-car garage." She looked up at him speculatively. "Are you really going to sue me?"

He chuckled as he steered the car off the tree-lined road onto a small dirt turn-off. As he reached for the parking brake Rose slid over toward the passenger-side door, poised for fight or flight.

"Huge, arrogant male?" he queried.

"Exactly. My mother warned me about men like you!"

"But you didn't pay any attention to the warning?"

"I'm not as smart as my mother was. What are you *doing*?"

"This is called kissing, Rosie." And he proceeded to demonstrate.

After which Rosie said, "That's not fair. If I were as big and as strong as you are you wouldn't get away with that."

"If you were as big and as strong as I am, Rosie, I wouldn't have any compulsion at all to kiss you. But since you're small and soft and edible, and cuddly, why, I believe I'll have another serving." And he left her gasping for breath, fighting to control her temper.

"Well, about that suit?" she demanded.

"Strictly a nuisance suit," he told her. "He hasn't a leg to stand on. There's no doubt in my mind that any competent lawyer could prove he swindled the poor widow."

"So why don't you have him thrown in jail?"

"Because we're only talking about a modest sum. The widow lost about seven thousand dollars. When I throw the book at him I want it to knock him for six, not just give him a black eye."

"You mean you're looking for some other swindling he might have done?"

"Alleged to have done," he corrected her. "That's what we say in the legal profession. Alleged to have done."

"Even though—even though it's only a small swindle?"

"Even though. Do you know somebody from whom he's stolen a handful of change?"

"So to speak. Some bonds. He went into my bank and presented an authorization to sell some of my bonds."

"And he had no such authorization?"

"None at all. And he got the money in a cashier's check and I don't know what he's done with it."

"Small change? You bother me when you talk about money, Rosie. Just how much was it?"

"Four hundred and fifty-one thousand dollars. Not counting four years' worth of compound interest."

"Holy Mother Mary," he yelled. He even scared the car. The motor choked and stopped. "Four hundred and—"

"Fifty-one thousand," she repeated.

He held up his hands in surrender. "And with no authorization?"

"I made him my broker on three of my accounts. In writing. He was only authorized to make recommendations to me. Instead, he closed out the account without a word to me. I don't dare to ask anybody about the other two. They were for *real* money."

"Don't tell me," he said, sighing. "I've had investigators snooping around after this guy for weeks, and it falls right into my lap. I have to think about this, Rosie."

"So okay, think," she told him, and then said, almost under her breath, "And don't call me Rosie!"

Sam Horton settled back against the driver's seat and restarted the engine. "Where is this Round Hill?"

"Straight ahead until you come to Hetty Green Street, then turn left again. It's what used to be the estate of Colonel Green, Hetty's only son. She was one of the real Wolfs of Wall Street. Her son Ned spent it almost as fast as she could make it. The Colonel owned a railroad in Texas. And a couple dozen or more other things in other places. It was back in the era of railroads and magnates, J. P. Morgan, Vanderbilt, and Ned Green! And there—that's the house he built."

"Colonel Green? A veteran?"

"Not exactly. I'm not sure, but the way I hear it he was commissioned in the Texas militia. Or some such thing. There really wasn't much he could do. He was a cripple. One of his legs became infected when he was a child and his mother refused to do anything about it. She was the one who inherited the whaling fortune; and then she went into the stock market and built it up into something substantial.

"He had a lot of interests. Back in the days of the first radio stations he used to re-broadcast music and news from his house, and all the poor people from miles around would come out here in their cars and listen. He kept a yacht, and drove an electric automobile down to New Bedford. He also sponsored the old whaling ship, the *Charles W. Morgan*, and had it set up as a tourist attraction right over there." Rose pointed out across the bay. "He was a sort of Renaissance man, people tell me. The *Morgan* is gone now, transferred to Connecticut, where they made an outdoor museum of all kinds of ships."

They had come to the gate leading into Round Hill—a guarded gate. Sam took a look at the armed guards and sighed. "Admission only to members?" Rose did her best to hide her smirk. "You could have said."

"You didn't want me to be right."

"That's not quite true," Sam said, aggrieved. "I didn't want me to be wrong! This is all I get to see?"

"I brought my opera glasses," she told him as she reached into her purse and pulled out the little binoculars. "You can see the big house that the Colonel built. Three floors, granite and marble. Sixty rooms. The Colonel sponsored a good many young ladies—he called them his 'wards'. But then, before he died, he up and married his housekeeper. Anyway, after his death developers made the main house into a condominium, and then built more very expensive new houses."

"Looks like a real baronial English mansion," Sam commented as he scanned the area. "Left it all to his wife, I suppose?"

"Not so's you'd notice. The Colonel and his mother had a big thing about government and taxes. She used to trade on the stock market but never opened an office. She did all her trading from a collapsible table and chair in the outer lobby of her New York bank."

"Sounds a little dumb to me."

"To me too, believe me. But we're talking turn-of-the-century real money, you know. When the Colonel's mother, Hetty, died she left something in the order of a hundred million dollars. When the Colonel died about half of it was disbursed for inheritance taxes, and all the rest went to the Colonel's sister, Sylvia."

"And then what?"

"Well, the first thing that Sylvia did was to order the Colonel's wife, Mable—formerly his housekeeper, you remember—to vacate the premises. And she went. Which left a large number of gossips to believe that the Colonel never really married her. How about that?"

"And that's the end of the story?"

"Not quite. The developers planned to fence off one of the finest beaches in New England, but the town of Dartmouth stepped in, seized the beaches by right of eminent domain, and that's it. The end of the great whaling fortune and the Green family. All gone now."

"Interesting. Now, about this wedding of ours. I had thought we might rent a piece of Round Hill and live it up, but I see that's not feasible."

"Not for anything less than four million. 'About'? You're changing your mind about the wedding?" Don't make it sound all that important, she told herself. Be a little casual. Just because it's everything in the world to you, it doesn't mean it has to be the same for him.

The front seat of his van comprised one long bench that ran from door to door. He untangled his long legs from the gears and slid over next to her. His right arm came around her and pulled her tightly against him.

"You've changed your mind?" she repeated. One of his big fingers tilted her chin up and over to his direction.

"Tears in your eyes, Rosie? No, I haven't changed *my* mind. Have you?" He leaned down and kissed each of her leaky orbs.

"No," she managed to say. "I—haven't changed my mind."

"That's good," he said. "Now the next question is—when?"

"I don't know," she said, sighing. "I had a big wedding once—flowers and preaching and all—at St. Peter's."

"I would want Penny to be in on this, love. It's very important. And I don't think she'll be out of the hospital for some time."

"I *said* I *had* one of those," Rose said. "I don't need another." One of her fists dug at her eye and managed to dislodge another loose tear. And left her eye all red and runny. "I don't have any family," she added. She looked up at him inquisitively.

"I have a father and a mother and three brothers," he said. "My father and mother live in Boston. My brothers are scattered over half the earth."

"Then how about Tuesday?" she suggested, trembling for fear of rejection. Lord, she thought, listen to me. Whatever happened to Little Miss Tough Kid? "We could ask your father and mother to come down to the hospital to visit, and I'll ask the Reverend Halfman to join us, and we can get married at Penny's bedside."

"Rosie, that's it," he said, smiling broadly. "But I won't invite the doctor. He charges so much per hour that even you couldn't afford it."

"If I keep on the way I'm going, I won't be able to afford the minister's fee," she said, and wiped her eye again. "What am I going to do about Chad Westbrook? And don't call me Rosie!"

"First of all," he said slowly, "if he has any more of your funds in hand we're going to discharge him. Fire him. Kick him out!"

"He has," Rose said. "You make that sound as if you might enjoy it."

He gave her another little hug. "Enjoy what?"

"Kicking him out," she said. "That would be a real pleasure, but he's ever so big, Sam."

"Don't think I haven't noticed," he said, chuckling. He glanced at his wristwatch. "C'mon, kid. We have an appointment in New Bedford."

* * *

Penny was propped up in bed when they arrived. The nurse who was specialing her case nodded to them both, picked up her knitting, and said, "I'll be out in the lounge. She's one tough little lady. Tells me she has to be because her mother expects it of her."

"It was 'sposed to be a secret," Penny said indignantly. "That's my mom. Pretty, ain't she?"

"*Isn't* she," Sam corrected her.

"And that's my dad," Penny went on. "He's some kind of a stick, but ya hafta expect that with lawyers. Do you need a lawyer? We need the business."

"Penelope Horton!"

"And now he's mad at you," the nurse said, chuckling. "I'll be back and you can tell me some more about your adventures in the Arctic." She rolled up her knitting, tucked it under the table, winked at the adult company, and went out of the ward door and into the hall.

"Adventures in the Arctic?" her father said.

"She's a nice lady," Penny said firmly. "I hadta do somethin' to entertain her, didn't I? What would you have done, Mom?"

"Probably just what you did," Rose conceded as she leaned over the bed and kissed the child on her forehead. "There now, not much temperature left. How does your leg feel?"

"I guess it must be okay," Penny said. "I don't really feel nothin', except it's hard to move around, and I have to sleep on my back. I hate that. Do you sleep on your back, Mom?"

Rose blushed. "No, I can't say that I do," she admitted. "I sleep sort of cuddled up, you know."

"My dad snores."

"Penelope!"

"Well, she has to find out some time or another. And you do, you know. Do you snore, Mom?"

"No, I'm sure I don't," Rose replied. "I had a person once who claimed that I did, so I stayed awake several nights in a row, and didn't catch myself snoring a single snore."

"Well, you won't hafta bother for the first few nights, I betcha!"

"Now that's what makes me—" Her father coughed and cleared his throat. "I wish I could find a school," he said, "that would teach my daughter reading, writing and arithmetic, and let *me* teach her about sex and solicitude."

"Do you know anything about that?" his daughter enquired, and only the appearance of the doctor saved her father from a stroke.

"Ah, there you are, Mr. Horton. Good. And Mrs. Horton?"

"Soon to be," Penny interjected.

"Next Tuesday," Rose said.

"Good for you all," the doctor said. "After careful considerations we have decided that Penelope requires only one hip replacement, and if you're all agreeable I would propose to do that next Wednesday."

"*We*?" Rose asked.

"We." The doctor brushed back the white lock that fell over his forehead. "The four of us, that is. Not the imperial we." He turned to Penny. "We'll start early in the morning and be finished in a couple of hours, and that will be the end of that!"

"But not the end of me?" Penny asked anxiously. Rose leaned over the bed and hugged the child gently, then kissed her again.

"Not a chance," the doctor assured her. "And after the operation there'll be two or three months of therapy—"

"What's that mean?" Penny interrupted.

"Exercises," he said. "Exercises, young lady. Walking instead of talking. Swimming. Things like that."

Penny pursed her lips. "I think I'd druther hear more about the wedding," she said. "But I'm too tired tonight."

CHAPTER EIGHT

"PENNY was looking well, didn't you think?" Sam asked the following Monday evening as he ushered her into his van in the hospital parking lot.

"Yes, but tired," Rose replied. "And what with the wedding tomorrow, then the operation on Wednesday... Poor kid." She squirmed around, trying to get comfortable on the high seat. "It's ten o'clock, and way past my bedtime. Millie will be worried about me."

"Worried? Bedtime? Look at that moon, lady. Full moon, clear skies, hardly any wind, and you're twenty-seven years old. You could easily stay out later, if you were of a mind to."

"What are you suggesting?"

"Not what you think. Tell me about Westbrook." Rose looked up at him in surprise. "How come you only guessed that he had a three- or four-car garage?"

"Because I've never been inside his house," Rose said indignantly. "Just what kind of a girl do you think I am, Sam Horton?"

"I think you're a very nice girl," he said, grinning down at her. "Was he as good at kissing as I am?"

"In about two shakes of a lamb's tail I'm going to beat up on you," she muttered. "I never tried to find out. I was never attracted to him in that way."

Horton had been sitting up straight in his seat, both hands on the steering wheel. At her answer he relaxed, settled back in the cushions, and sighed a massive sigh. "Well, thank the Lord for that," he said. "I never was

135

much of a one for love matches. For others, that is. Now, let's get down to business.''

"What business? What are you driving at?"

"What sort of cars does he have in this four-car garage of his?"

"I'm not sure, exactly. He has one of those low-slung Italian cars. And he has a Rolls. That's an antique car, by the way. He only brings it out for special events.'' She ran a hand through her hair and puzzled at something. "For that matter I haven't seen his Italian car in a long time, if that means anything. And then he has one of those new Cherokee Jeeps—and I don't know what the other one might be. Some sort of American sedan, I think. And just what are you getting at?"

"Idle curiosity," he murmured. "The moon ought to be down in another hour, wouldn't you say?"

"Just about," she acknowledged. "So?"

"It was nice down there on Round Hill. Be nicer now, I suspect. The ghost of the old Colonel is probably haunting the area. And I'll bet he has a passion for young lovers.''

"He? He's been dead for almost a quarter century. And neither one of us is a particularly *young* lover.''

"Hey there. Just a minute," he said. "You're twenty-seven—''

"Twenty-eight next month," she interrupted.

"So going on twenty-eight—''

"And you?"

"Would you believe I'm thirty-four, going on thirty-five?" he asked her. "Okay, so how about middle-aged love?''

"I'm not *that* old," she said indignantly. "Just what do you have in mind?"

"Well, I thought we might drive back to Smith Neck Road and neck a little—''

"Boy, you have to be older than thirty-four," she interjected. "Necking went out in the sixties."

"The word went out, the doing didn't," he corrected her. "And we can't sit in this parking lot necking, because here comes the security guard."

"What am I going to do with the likes of you?" she asked glumly.

"Marry me," he offered. "Isn't that the plan?"

"Come on," she said. "Let's go down to Smith Neck and neck."

"That's my girl."

The hospital security guard stopped walking toward them as soon as Sam turned on his lights, and the officer waved to them as the van ponderously made its way out of the narrow parking lot.

"Now what?" he asked as they turned south and headed toward Padanaram.

"Dartmouth Street," she instructed. "Find the bridge. Cross it until you come to Smith Neck Road—"

"All right," he said. "I know the rest. Why are you sitting so far away from me?"

"Safety precaution. I don't trust wolves running in the dark of night."

"The moon's still out," he observed. "There are plenty of lights—from South Dartmouth, Padanaram—what did you say the name of that little settlement is?"

"Nonquit."

"Yeah. Nonquit. Indian name?"

"Most unusual places in town are Indian names. Wampanoag tribe, for the most part."

"A big tribe?"

"Not really. Most of them live out on the islands. Gay Head is the tribal center."

"That's the tribe that hopes to open a gambling casino in New Bedford?"

"Yes. So they hope. The federal government supports the right of all the tribes to set up gambling casinos if they wish. After all, the tribes are all independent nations, and except for a few treaty items they're welcome to do whatever they please."

"Where the devil are we going?" she asked suddenly.

"Down into Nonquit," he said. "Nice name. I thought I'd give it the once-over. And over to the beach. According to my map we could park near King Philip Road and watch the moon go down. Move over a little closer, Rosie. King who?"

"King Philip. When the Pilgrims first came to this area Massasoit was the local chief. He treated the whites well. But by the time his son took over the tribe things weren't going so well. King Philip, that was. There was a bloody war. And don't call me Rosie!"

"I'll humor you for a while," he said, "but after the wedding I'll call you whatever I like, and you'll answer to it. Right?"

"Just drive," she said.

"And it's possible there might be a war right here tonight." And then he just drove, whistling some impossible tune between his teeth.

"You can't drive this way!" she exclaimed. "Didn't you see the signs? This is all private property—the whole of Nonquit is open only to the resident owners."

"Then I can't stop here," he said. "That house is marked 'Superintendent of Nonquit'. Look at those houses, will you?"

"I've looked," she said. "The whole place was built as a private summer resort. In the old days those houses used to go at one hundred thousand. Nowadays some of them are worth half a million."

"And dig the fancy golf course," he added. "And tennis courts— Lord, you'd have to be a millionaire to live in a place like this. And Westbrook has a house here?"

"Yes. He inherited it. Besides which it's almost outside the corporate boundaries."

"How about that? Out in the poverty zone?"

While he talked he was guiding the big van at speed down the narrow, winding roads, until finally the sea was in front of them. He pulled up beside a rocky patch just outside the fence that marked off the Nonquit boundary. Dead ahead, lit by the remaining moonlight, was the outer realm of Apponaganset Bay. The offshore breeze was piling up whitecaps which crashed against the beach and ran up on the sand for several feet. One sixty-foot sailcraft was speeding its way along the far horizon, heading for Padanaram harbor. Its running lights outlined the vessel and the sea.

To their left a few lights gleamed in houses within the colony. To their right a dead-end road pointed toward the distant microwave antennae at Round Hill. Alongside the dead-end road was a low-level marsh, sprinkled with shadowy wild pink roses. And still further back, outside the Nonquit boundary, two or three large houses were perched on the bluffs.

Rose inhaled the saltiness of the sea and settled back, a dreamy, pleased smile on her face.

"You love the sea," he murmured. Not a question, but a flat statement.

"Who could not?" she said. "I've lived by the ocean all my born days. I made a trip to Las Vegas once. People say that the desert out there is something to see. I couldn't hurry fast enough to get back to the smell of salt water and my ocean."

"So that rules out our living in Ohio," he said, chuckling. "But you wouldn't have liked the spring floods anyway. And Penny's afraid of them."

"I don't blame her." At just that moment the moon settled low in the western sky behind the trees and dropped out of sight. Darkness plunged down on them, and only the artificial lights made marks in the area.

Rose shivered and moved an inch or two closer to him. His arm came over her shoulders. She rested her russet head against his shoulder.

The night wasn't really cold. Rose Mary just felt nervous. After all, what did she really know about this man? He was a man of many intents, and while she meant to cast her life into his hands she couldn't help but feel a residual touch of fear.

He switched off the car lights and slid over closer to her. Both of his arms came around her and squeezed gently. The tiny specks of doubt fled, scattered by the warmth of his love. She moaned, a little, and settled her chin against his collar.

"Something wrong, darling?"

"No. Something right," she said as she squeezed in closer.

Silence. The smell of roses mixed with the salt of the sea. One or two sea birds, lost in the dark, screamed. A burst of gaiety pierced the night.

"Party?"

"Probably," Rose said. "They do a lot of partying over here."

"So tell me, where does Westbrook live?"

She squirmed around in his arms and pointed out the back window. "That one," she said. "The blue one up on the bluff."

"Ah." He's like Millie, Rose told herself. She says a lot of "ah"s too. "I just wonder where Mr. Wonderful might be tonight. Any idea?"

"Mr. Wonderful?"

"Your Mr. Westbrook."

"I've told you and told you. He's not *my* Mr. Westbrook. And as far as I know he's out of town. According to the New Bedford paper he's down in New York attending a brokers' conference. He'll be gone until tomorrow."

"Very dependable, this newspaper?"

"Pretty much so. And Chad spends a lot of time making sure he gets his name in the paper correctly. Why do you ask?"

"Pucker up," he said. "One more kiss and then we'll get to work."

Rose was a happy participant. No matter what the mystery, she was more than willing to share a kiss. Or two. Or three.

"And now we'll go to work," Sam said eventually.

"Not me," she said firmly. "I don't intend to stir a finger until you tell me just what the devil you're up to."

"Oh, Lord," he muttered. "What ever happened to love, honor and obey?"

"That went out years ago," she informed him. "Love and honor you might break even with, but obey disappeared with Queen Victoria. Try again."

"You're a hard-hearted woman, Rose Mary," he grumbled.

"Never mind all that, Sam Horton. Just a simple explanation will do, starting about now."

"If you think I'm going to be hen-pecked, Rose, you've got another think coming!"

"So I'll take another think," she snapped. "Explain. All these powers and platitudes you're feeding me don't go into gear until *after* the ceremony. I've told you that once before."

"Well," he started out slowly, "my youngest brother, Henry, was born with a multitude of physical problems. Although my dad was a banker he could hardly keep his head above water. So when I decided to go to college and law school the question was where would the money come from."

"I follow. You could talk a little faster if you want to do something before dawn."

"Not even a word of sympathy, Rose?"

"Sympathy? I love you, Sam. Why would you need sympathy? What's the rest of the story?"

"Why indeed?" he said. "I worked my way through."

"Both college and law school?"

"Both. Just listen, will you?"

"I will," she promised. "What kind of work?"

"To begin with I worked as an apprentice to a private investigator."

"A PI? That must have been exciting!"

"There's no more boring work in the world," Sam said. "But I learned a lot and it caused me to think a lot. Now, what would be the first thing you'd look for in a hit-and-run auto case?"

"I don't know," Rose answered. "I don't have that sort of mind."

"So I'll tell you. First you gather up all the physical evidence you can find, and then you look for the car that matches—paint, scrapings, dents—everything."

"But the police have done all that."

"So then you go into the records. You find the list of possible cars, and then find out which of them haven't been seen on the streets lately."

"Oh, my God!" Rose exclaimed.

"Yes?"

"Chad Westbrook. He had an Italian car, a Ferrari. He was very proud of it. And then, after—but that doesn't apply to Penny."

"But it *does* apply to your husband. To Frank."

"And I've never seen his Ferrari since—the day that Frank was killed."

"And according to my investigator he didn't sell it, and he doesn't seem to me to be the kind of fellow who would junk it."

Rose climbed out of the car and looked up at the big blue house and its four-car garage. "So where would he put it?" she mused. "Inside his great big garage, locked and covered?"

"Now you're thinking, Rosie." He held up both hands. "No, I know; don't call you Rosie."

"You may call me anything you want," she said as she jumped at him and threw her arms around his neck, "just so long as we can find that car. What do we do now? Get a search warrant or something?"

"Not a chance, Rosie. That's the way honest people do it. And it gets them nowhere. One of the things I learned is how to break into houses and garages and places like that. Shall we?"

"And if we get caught?"

"It's a long way from here to New York, and if we get caught I'll think of something. Shall we give it a try?"

"Love, honor and cherish. At least for tonight," she said, grinning at him. "You're a lawyer, and you want me to break the law? Why don't we just go and get a search warrant?"

"Can't be done," he said. "This is a real catch 22. The evidence we need to get a search warrant is inside that garage. There's no way we can convince a judge to give us a search warrant until we get the information that's inside. So, honest citizens are completely barred. There are only two ways to go. First, we might trick brother Chad into leaving the doors open, which is a difficult problem. Or second, we go up there and open the doors ourselves."

"Then what? We go before the judge and say, 'Dear Judge, we just happened to think that the evidence was in his garage, so we just couldn't help but break in—in the nighttime—and there it was. So now if you'll give us a search warrant we'll go back and get the evidence?' "

"Lady, you're a hard one to do business with," he muttered. "Why don't you go sit by the seaside while I—?"

"Why don't we go up there and set fire to the house?" she suggested. "Then sooner or later the fire department will come. They can legally break in, can't they?"

She looked up at him, her head slightly tilted, like a bird peering at him from a branch.

"Say, that's a great idea," he said sarcastically. "Then the police will come along with the firemen, they'll arrest us for arson, and throw our lovable little butts in the jailhouse for five hundred years. Less time off for good behavior—if any."

"But—"

"But I bet that a cheapskate like Westbrook has only a cheap padlock on the garage door. If we don't steal anything, the most they can charge us with is the value of a ten-dollar padlock. If you don't have a criminal record the most that can happen is a probationary sentence. Trust me, lady."

"All right," she said dolefully. "What do you suppose my mother would say?"

"Hell, how would I know? What do you think Millie would say?"

They both knew what Millie would say. In fact, what actual words she would use. Even a husky man like Sam Horton shuddered at the thought. But then there was Penny to consider.

"There's a road that goes around back of the hill," she said. "You have to drive all the way through Nonquit, and—"

"And half the community would notice," he retorted. "C'mon, girl, we're going walking."

"Through the swamp?" Rose clamped both hands over her mouth.

"There aren't any alligators this far north," he said. Which was not exactly comforting to a woman who feared a number of other things besides alligators.

He opened the side door of the van and took out a camera. "Carry this," he ordered, "while I park the van under those trees over there. I'm sure they have some sort of patrol during the night."

Dazed, Rose grabbed at the camera and stepped aside while he smartly backed the vehicle under cover. When he climbed out of the driver's seat he was wearing some sort of tool belt around his waist.

The walk turned into an all-out hike. Three quarters of an hour later they climbed up out of the swamp and onto cleared ground. Rose was wet to the knees, and a musky smell haunted her. Only the fact that he was holding her hand kept her on her feet. In the meager light of the moon, and at a time when most electric lights had been turned off, she could barely see the outline of Westbrook's house before she bumped into the side of the garage door.

"Shh," Sam hissed.

"Shh, yourself," she muttered. "If Chad is in New York how can he hear me?"

"You're just *guessing* he's in New York," he replied. "And besides, there's another house about a hundred yards from here. And with my luck they'll have a dog."

"Don't say that," she demanded. Her shoes were full of water. He began examining the door, so she sat down on the gravel and took both of them off to drain.

"Damn," he muttered.

"Don't say that," she snapped. "There might be dogs! What's the matter?"

"It's not a simple padlock," he mumbled as he fished around in his tool belt. A couple of screwdrivers clinked against each other. Not a loud noise, by any means, but in her present state Rose could have been startled by the tearing of two paper tissues.

"Don't do that," she snapped. She was still sitting on the gravel, giving thanks for her blue jeans.

"I'm not doing anything," he returned. "The damn lugs won't turn."

"You'd do better if you paid attention to what you're doing," she returned, "and stopped trying to lick my ear."

"Lick your—what?"

"I don't think I'll ever come to understand you," Rose said, with a huge sigh. She looked up at him, shifted her seat slightly, and was rewarded with another lick. He was outlined against the big white garage door by the flashing light of a distant harbor buoy. Outlined. All of him.

"Sam," she half whispered.

"Just a minute. I'm almost finished here."

"Sam—do you like dogs? Big dogs?"

"All depends." There was a moment of silence. "There it is. What sort of big dogs?"

"I was thinking about the German kind. Rottweilers, I think they're called."

"Nice animals," he commented. "Not usually too friendly, but nice animals. Why would you ask a silly question like that?"

"B-because." It was hard to keep her lip from trembling.

"All right, I'll bite—"

"No. Don't even make that suggestion," she gasped.

For the first time he noticed the tremor in her voice. The tools at his waist tinkled briefly. His outline shifted as he bent over in her direction.

"I wouldn't do that," she cautioned. "There's this big, heavy dog with his head on my lap and I'm afraid that—"

His outline paused, halfway down. "Oh, Lord," he muttered. "Why is it that the only luck I've had lately has all been bad?"

"Don't say that!"

"Why not? He's probably the dog from the house next door. Disturb him and he'll bark his head off. Just before he tries to eat us, of course."

"He—doesn't have a collar, Sam." Her fingers were gently exploring, running up and down the bag of bones which was the dog's body, caressing his neck, ruffling his matted fur just behind his ear. "And he feels as if he hasn't eaten in days."

"Well, let's hope he doesn't decide to practise on us," Sam said. "I'm not all that comfortable with dogs. Can you keep him under control?"

"I suppose. He's either trying to lick my hand or bite a sample. So there *is* something you're afraid of!"

"Besides you, you mean?"

"He's soaking wet, Sam. Don't be sarcastic. Oh, the poor dear. I don't suppose you have anything in your pockets he could eat?"

"Nothing but my hands, Rosie. Come on, now. We've finished the *breaking* part; now all we have to do is the *entering*."

He bent over again in her direction. The dog growled.

"Now that's enough, Rudolph," she commanded. The dog managed to work his way up onto his four feet, whined politely and bounced his heavy tail off her legs a time or two. Sam's hand caught up Rosie's and gently tugged her to her feet.

"Rudolph?" Sam queried. "Lean against this side panel. The door flips up—I think. Why Rudolph?"

Rose moved to one side and rested a shoulder against the garage timbers. "It's the only sensible name to use," she retorted. "First because it's an imperial name, secondly because the poor fellow is barely a skeleton. Third, because he came with us to Chad's house, and lastly because Chad's full name is Chadwick Rudolph West-brook. And he's—"

"I know," Sam interrupted. "And he's as miserable as his namesake."

"Now if you'll kindly open the door," she said primly.

Although the lock was unfastened, the door was not really prepared to rise up and shine. Sam set both feet firmly on the concrete lip of the entryway and pulled his mightiest. The door squeaked and groaned. The dog whined. Rose crossed her fingers, and finally the door swung up on its gimbal pins and slid into the ceiling slots provided for it.

"Thank God, Rosie," Sam said. "Next time you see him, tell your boyfriend to use a little oil, huh?"

"I'll be sure to tell him," she said curtly. "Don't call me Rosie. How are we supposed to see in the dark?"

"My Boy Scout training stands us in good stead," he said, chuckling. "This modern innovation is called a flashlight."

A tiny beam of light split the darkness; the dog whined and crowded behind Rose's legs, shivering. She bent to comfort the animal.

"That was more noise than I expected," Sam said as he walked out into the open and looked anxiously to either side. Not a light lit, not a person moved, not a dog barked. He came back inside the stuffy, mildewed garage.

"Smells as if he hasn't aired the place out in months," he muttered. He flashed the tiny beam of light around in a generous circle. "Three cars."

"There ought to be four," Rose whispered. Now that the initial work was done she felt a little thrill of accomplishment. "I don't see the Ferrari."

"We can't spend a lot of time wondering," Sam said. "There may be an alarm, or a police patrol. Places like this—"

"Are summer resorts," Rose reminded him. "And there isn't a single policeman anywhere in Nonquit. The nearest station is over in Dartmouth, and I think there's only one police car there. We've had to cut the budget this year."

"Yeah," Sam said as he moved toward the Rolls-Royce. "Look at this beauty, will you? Must be twenty-five years old and everything shines. He must spend hours with a polishing cloth."

"Not Chadwick," Rose retorted. "If it's polished he hired someone to do the polishing. In all the years I've known him I've never seen Chad Westbrook raise a drop of perspiration."

"Why should he when he knows people like you?" Sam said.

"Sarcasm will get you nowhere," she muttered. "And it makes a cold bed on a dark night."

"Well, this Rolls hasn't been engaged in hit-and-run warfare," he said. "A cold bed?" He tugged her over to his side. "Is there a message there somewhere?"

Rose, who knew a thing or two these days that she hadn't known before she'd met Sam, was no longer afraid to admit it, relaxed against him. "The trouble with you," she said, "is me. The only way I can maintain a proper perspective is to be more than two feet away from you."

"Too bad you can't maintain your distance," he said, pulling her even closer. Rudolph whined nervously, and when she paid him no attention the dog stood up on his hind legs with his forepaws on her shoulder and wagged his tail.

Rose found herself, again, unable to resist Sam's appeal. Look at me, God, she thought. My jeans are old and ragged, and their seat is wet. My blouse is fit for the Good Will collections—as dust rags. My hair has been blowing in the wind for hours and looks like a bird's nest. Why would any man want me?

When I get back to Padanaram I'm going to take a lot of money out of the bank and I'm going to go up to Boston and shop my way into beauty. I know money can do it. And in the meantime, as long as he *does* want me, I don't intend to disabuse him of that crazy idea—not for all the tea in China.

So she moved up on tiptoes, pursed her lips and waited. And he kissed her, knowing full well that this was the only woman who could share his life. The woman for whom he would make all sacrifices. The woman who would make his daughter whole and happy. So he kissed her again, softly, gently, rising on a wind of passion from the level of comfort and concern to that immeasurable height which only love could reach.

And after a time and time again, when they broke free to breathe, he said, "There is no Ferrari, love. Why do you insist on a Ferrari?"

Rose shrugged. "It was only a wild chance. There was paint on Frank's wheelchair. The police laboratory said that it was Italian paint, of the style used mainly on a Ferrari. I knew Chad had an Italian car of that make, and I've looked for months at every Italian car driving down the street. But if there isn't one here there isn't one. I believe what our priest told me—that although whoever killed Frank is able to conceal his crime from us he cannot conceal it from God."

"You're a brave woman, Rose Mary," he said softly. "And not everything is lost. That second car is an American Buick sedan. I don't see any damage to it. And the third car is a Jeep.

"Damn. My flashlight batteries are running out. But look quickly at that car over in the corner." He moved the focus of his light over in that direction.

"I can't tell," Rose said, almost crying. "It's covered by a tarpaulin."

Sam took her by the arm and walked her over to the covered car. "Low-slung," he said as he whipped the cover off. "Two-seater. Four-cylinder. Broken right headlight. Scarred right fender. A British Triumph."

"And the right color," she added. "Penny!"

"Help me scrape some of this paint off," he said as his hands moved busily. "And perhaps some of that broken glass from the headlight. And while you do that I'll take a dozen pictures."

"Is that going to help? You said we couldn't use anything for evidence."

"But we can give the police enough for them to get a search warrant. And the only thing remaining is for us to put everything back in order so that Westbrook can't tow the car away when we're not looking."

"Some good will come of it," she murmured as she helped out. "God will not be mocked!"

"Nor Sam Horton, either," he said as he pounded one of his fists against his leg.

She looked at him, aghast. "S-Sam," she stuttered. "'Vengeance is mine...saith the Lord.'"

"Yes," he said grimly. "But I don't go to *that* church!"

CHAPTER NINE

TUESDAY September the thirteenth, nine o'clock in the morning. Your wedding day, Rose Mary Chase, she thought as she struggled to open her eyes. In six hours Rose Mary Chase would become Rose Mary Horton. And the next time she snuggled into a bed she would no longer be alone. Rose shivered deliciously at the thought. There was a certain savor to being married for the second time. There would be no more virginal fears. Everything would be as it ought to be.

In the little time they had had to talk it over, it had been decided that they would consolidate their little families in the old Chase household on Middle Street at the corner of Bridge. The Horton house, up one block on the corner of Franklin, would be offered for sale. At Rose's house there were more rooms, and a swimming pool in the backyard for Penny's exercises. The house already had an elevator, so Penny would have more freedom to come and go. And the master bedroom would be—masterful.

Millie, standing in the doorway, cleared her throat. Rose rolled over, smiled and put her feet on the floor.

"Don't hurry, love. I've brought your breakfast."

"I could come down, Millie."

"Not a chance," the elderly housekeeper said. "The bride has her breakfast in bed. Then she dresses ever so slowly, and at two o'clock we go down to the hospital. When are Sam's parents coming in?"

"They're already here. They came in last night and put up at the Day's Inn down near Route Six. We'll meet at the hospital."

"He kept you out pretty late last night. And your shoes are a wreck. Mud on everything."

"Would you believe I fell into a swamp?"

"Probably not, but it hardly matters. How do you like this dress?"

Millie held it up on its hanger for examination. "Nice," Rose said. It was plain ivory, knee-length, with a jeweled collar, a translucent upper bodice and a full skirt that flared out from her full hips, padded by a crinoline petticoat to provide a little "swish" to the afternoon's entertainment.

Rose was struck by it all, but wanted to be practical. "A full zipper in the back?" she asked.

"As ordered," Millie reported. "Somehow I get the feeling that you're more interested in getting *out* of it than you are about getting *in*."

"A girl has to be considerate of the groom's feelings," Rose said primly.

"You mean he *ordered* the zipper?"

"Well, for the first couple of weeks I intend to be—er—compliant," Rose stated firmly. "Then I'll put his nose to the grindstone. First I have to get Penny under control, you understand, and then I can take Sam into training."

"Dream on," Millie said, laughing. "Eat your breakfast. You'll need your strength."

"Millie!"

"Not to worry, Rose Mary. The master bedroom has been cleaned and polished to a fare-thee-well. Penny will be in the blue room on the opposite side of the house. The stair elevator has been checked out and oiled, and the refrigerator is stuffed to the top. The men from the electronic place are downstairs working on the intercom system. Where are you going on your honeymoon?"

"He hasn't told me yet. By the way, did you feed Rudolph this morning?"

"You mean that mangy dog who was hiding under the stove in the kitchen? He looks as if he hasn't eaten in a dog's age. Rudolph?"

"Well, it seemed appropriate at the time. We'll have to take him to the vet's as soon as we can. How is he getting along with the cats?"

"I think he's afraid of the mother cat, but the two kittens seem to think his ears are ideal for practice. By the time Rudolph gets fed up to full strength, they should all be settled down."

"Don't be too sure," Rose said. "Once Rudolph is fed up to fighting weight he'll be the terror of the block. I think."

"All interesting," Millie agreed. "Incidentally, I hear that WXBN is going to broadcast the marriage rites."

"They *what*!"

"They're going to broadcast your wedding ceremony. Your groom put them up to it."

"He did?" Rose said weakly. "What's this—oatmeal? You know I never— Oh, well, it can't last for long. But it does seem as if the world's been turned upside down."

"And where is your loving groom this morning?"

"I'm darned if I know. He said he had things to do, and the bride and groom shouldn't see each other until the ceremony. Does that sound a little phoney to you, Millie?"

"Quite the custom, Rose. Normally the groom goes out 'with the boys' the night before the wedding. If he did he might need a few hours to recover. Did he?"

"Did he what?"

"Need time to recover?"

"I don't have that much experience with men," Mrs Rose Chase said.

Sam Horton was busy indeed. After sleeping late—but not as late as Rose—he called the hospital for his usual check on Penny, and talked to her for a few minutes.

His mother and father were at the child's bedside, and he included them in the conversation as well, but there were things to be done. He stopped by the Dartmouth mall and picked up the photographs.

"Best I've seen in years," the attendant told him. "It's hard to get good clear photos in a dark—er—garage?"

"A matter of practice," Sam said, avoiding the question. "Bait for a law case, you know." He very carefully put two copies of each photograph in large envelopes, and then addressed the envelopes to the Dartmouth police, the district attorney, and the state police. "The messengers are available now?" he asked the store manager.

"Ready and waiting," he was told. "All three packages will be delivered before noontime."

As a thank-you, Sam attached a ten-dollar bill to the outside of each envelope with a paper clip. Then back to his car and down Route Six to the Dartmouth post office he went.

"We have all sizes of envelopes," the woman at the desk told him, and helped as he packaged six eight by ten color photos into one large envelope. And then he spent a minute or two at the small writing table in the outer lobby, adding the address. 'To the Attorney General, Commonwealth of Massachusetts. Eyes Only.' No return address, but containing a note as to where the pictures were taken, and to what case they referred.

The original woman clerk had left the desk; a thin elderly man stamped the envelope and assessed the charges. "Do not fold, spindle or mutilate," Sam added. The man nodded without even looking up, then stamped the envelopes vigorously. Sam took a big breath and sighed. He didn't really want any investigator to discover who had mailed the pictures. Or broken into the garage to take them!

"Worth every penny," he commented as the clerk finished the stamping.

"Right," the postal attendant said. "Too bad they don't pay us what *we're* worth." Which was a debate that Sam would have liked to avoid. He watched as the envelopes disappeared down the bag chute. And then he headed out the door, into the sunshine.

A little old lady, one hand filled with packages and the other with a cane, was struggling with the outer door. Sam turned around and helped her into the air-conditioned lobby. She thanked him profusely, and when Sam turned around he bumped into—Chadwick Westbrook.

"What a surprise," Chad said. "How are we coming on with our assault on Rose Mary Chase? I really need the money in a hurry."

"I've had a surprise," Sam returned.

"Surprise?"

"Yes, I have to give up the case. I would recommend you find a lawyer from New Bedford. There are plenty of them available."

"But not as cheap as you," Chad protested, giving the show away. "I'd rather have you handle the case."

"I can't do that," Sam replied. "I've discovered a qualification that makes me unable to represent you."

"Dear God," Chad remarked. "What qualification?"

"Marriage."

"Marriage? Why should that disqualify you from taking action against Rose Chase?"

"Because that's who I'm gonna marry," Sam said. "This afternoon at three o'clock. Wanna come?"

"Me?" Chad roared. "Me? Go to the marriage of that—that whore?" He was screaming loudly enough to be heard at the school across the street. Half a dozen cars stopped and rolled their windows down to hear. Chad ran his mouth down to a finish, and actually had a white froth on his lips.

"I wish you wouldn't say that," Sam said. A police car rolled up and joined the cortege on the street. "That's my girl you're talking about." All this was said in a soft, reasonable voice. "I'd hate to have to take some sort of physical action."

Chad, who was some six or seven inches taller than Sam, laughed. "You're going to take some physical action? What a laughter that is. Listen here, I'm happy to see you married up with that little—"

And that was the point when Sam Horton took one step forward so that Chad's much longer arms would not have an advantage. Sam's fists doubled, he smiled at Chad, and his arm came around in a massive left hook that drove directly into Chad's solar plexus.

The big man felt the air blow out of him in a masterful "whoof". He bent over slightly, both hands in front of him to protect himself. He blinked three or four times, surprised at something that had never happened to him in all his life. His fists moved weakly, as if challenging Sam to try again.

Sam counted gently up to five, and then, since Chadwick was still acting aggressively, squared his feet away and turned loose his massive blacksmith's right arm. Westbrook made a vague blocking gesture which had no effect. Sam's right fist sank deep into his stomach, the tall man straightened up and, with a vague look of disbelief on his face, collapsed on the cement sidewalk.

There was a rattle of applause from the nearer bystanders, but the two policemen in the patrol car evidently had no sense of humor. They came boiling out of their car, struggling to free their batons from their belts.

"Just stand still there," one of them yelled, waving his baton.

"Who, me?" Sam rammed both his hands into his pockets and settled back against the wall of the post office.

"Yes, you," the cop confirmed. "Turn around and face the building, feet back, hands on the wall."

Sam, who loved detective movies, assumed the position. "It's him you ought to be arresting," he said.

"That's right." The little old lady, who had finished her errand, was now standing in the door. "I heard that—person—make some nasty remarks about this nice man's fiancée."

"But this other guy threw the first punch. We both saw that." His partner had finished patting Sam down. "All right now. Hands behind your back. Put the cuffs on him, Bruce."

"What are you arresting me for?" Sam asked.

"Assault and battery. Come on. We'll take you back to the station."

"Good Lord," Sam sighed. "I'm in trouble again? Look, I have a wedding to go to this afternoon."

"I'm sure they can get along without you," the first cop said. "Duck your head and get in the back of the car."

"But that's the trouble," Sam said. "They can't get along without me. I'm the groom."

"Not to worry," the other cop said. "We can have you booked and bailed by three o'clock. Plenty of time. Bring along the other guy, Bruce."

"If I can move him," Bruce said. "Lord, what a big sucker he is."

"Yeah. And went down with two hits," his partner reminded him. "So be careful."

"Hey, it was all an accident," Sam said glumly. "Why would a little guy like me pick on a mountain like him?"

"I don't know why," the cop said. "Just keep cool. With a little luck you might be out on bail by three o'clock."

"Yeah, sure," Sam grumbled. He had just remembered that he had only five dollars in his wallet, and had left his checkbook at home.

Rose and Millie arrived by taxi at St. Luke's Hospital at about two o'clock. The wedding was an ill-kept secret. Whispers followed them down the halls, up in the elevator, to the lounge of the children's ward, where the ward nurse met them. Their driver had parked his car in a lot across the street from the hospital entrance, assuming without asking that he was invited. Rose was grateful. In a world full of mysteries there was nothing more pleasant than a very large, very male escort. Pete Wilkins was the ideal man for such a purpose.

The lounge was half-full. Visiting hours were almost complete, and small groups were making their goodbyes. Except for the elderly pair in the corner. Rose targeted them and went straight across the area to introduce herself. There was a tremor in the vicinity of her stomach. After all, one didn't meet one's in-laws without someone to introduce one, and there was no sign of Sam.

"Mrs. Horton?" she asked tentatively. The woman was almost as short as Rose herself, but well filled out, a sort of bouncy grandma with a beautiful smile. She wore her white hair short and curled, and had covered herself modestly in a calf-length gold dress. A necklace of pearls circled her throat.

The man beside her was slightly bent with age, gray-haired, with a face that bore a thousand marks of living. Even with his stoop he stood a good six feet four. He wore a three-piece suit that spelled "banker". Take them together on average, Rose thought, and you come out with Sam. His height, his strength, his humor.

"And this is my husband, Arthur," Mrs. Horton said. "Rose?"

Rose Mary, old-fashioned, well trained, made a small curtsy. But her prospective mother-in-law opened both arms and hugged her. "Rose Mary?" She looked up at her husband while still embracing Rose. "I told you so, Arthur. Petite. Isn't she beautiful?"

"Did you expect our son to pick anyone else?" Arthur said gruffly. There was a hint of a tear in his eye. His eldest son was marrying, and who would not have spared a tear? "Where is that rascal?"

"I—don't know exactly," Rose said. "He had some business to transact, and said he would meet me here at—" she held up her wrist, where her mother's watch still kept perfect time "—at—fifteen minutes ago."

"He must have been held up by something important," Mrs. Horton said.

And what's more important than our wedding? Rose thought. But then men don't always think the way you expect they might. If his mother isn't worried, why should I be?

So she introduced Millie, and Pete the taxi driver, and eventually the Reverend Father Francis Halfman, rector of St. Peter's church. The group sat down and began to exchange information, mostly about Sam. It included a photo of Sam Horton in his birthday suit, at three months of age, which his mother carried in her wallet. And, not to be outdone, his father produced a picture from his wallet showing Sam in his Little League uniform, standing on the pitcher's mound and glaring at the opposition.

"Never could stand to lose a game," Arthur explained. "That was a bad year. They lost ten out of twelve, I believe."

By now it was four o'clock, and Rose Chase was raising a terrible anger, and doing her best to keep it under control. Waiting at the altar? Isn't that what it's called? she asked herself. I'll kill the man!

The head nurse from the children's ward stuck her head in the door. "The child is getting very nervous," she announced. The entire group filed out and across the hall, where the end of visiting hours had pruned the crowd considerably.

Anxious Penny was propped up in her bed, her bottom lip broken where she had been chewing on it for the past half-hour. Rose leaned over to hug her.

"I thought you might have changed your mind," the girl said. "I would have killed him if he did something to break up the wedding!"

"Not me," Rose murmured. "I'm one of those girls who never give up. At almost twenty-eight where would I find another man like your father?"

"So where is he?" Penny asked.

"What a good question," Rose returned.

"I'm sure he'll be along in a few minutes," Mrs. Horton said, trying to "sooth the savage breast". "He never was much of a one for being on time, but he always came."

"How comforting," Rose said sarcastically. Millie squeezed her arm in reprimand.

"You want I should go downstairs and look around?" Pete asked. "It's a big hospital." And Rose, looking squarely in his eyes, could read, And when I find him and break his arm they'll fix it right up.

"Mrs. Chase," one of the nurses called. "There's a telephone call for you. You may take it at the nurses' station."

"May I indeed?" Rose said, irritated. She walked slowly down the ward to the nurses' station and picked up the telephone. The group surrounding Penny's bed watched. It was a short conversation, and Rose put the receiver down very emphatically before she walked back.

"You found him," Mr. Horton said. It was a flat sort of statement, as if he didn't know the answer and wasn't sure he wanted to know.

"I found him," Rose said grimly. "Where did I leave my purse?"

"Mama?" Penny said. There were tears in the little girl's eyes.

"Nothing important, love," Rose reported gently as she bent down and kissed the child's cheek. "Your father—I mean my fiancé—is in jail, and I have to go bail him out."

Pete drove her.

With so many charges involved, the prisoners had been transferred to the holding cells of the district court, and the district attorney, Mr. Gomez, had taken over the case. Half a dozen people were waiting for her when she arrived.

"Mrs. Horton?" The district attorney for Bristol County was a man of the law, but also an elected politician. Seeing how angry this particular citizen was, he trod the waters carefully.

Rose consulted her watch. It was five o'clock. "Not exactly," she said. "I might have been at three o'clock this afternoon, but—"

"Yes," Gomez said, "and I recognize that part of the delay was due to my office. But, you see, we couldn't get in touch with the attorney general."

"The attorney general?" Rose gasped. "What has he done to warrant that kind of—persecution?"

"Bring him in," Gomez ordered. "I wanted to apologize before you saw him. I hope you understand."

"I don't understand anything," Rose said firmly. "Anything. Now, if there's someone here who might explain it all, I'd be very grateful. And maybe I could explain it then to the Democratic Committee of Dartmouth, of which I happen to be the vice chairperson."

Gomez decided to bow out at this point. "I have to run," he said. "I'm due in court." And he was gone.

But as he went out one door Sam Horton came in the other. "Hi, sweetheart," he said, smiling his best smile. "So they finally called you?"

He held out his arms to her, but Rose was angry enough to stay in place. "Yes, that's just what they did," she said coolly. "I really didn't mind. The wedding was already over-late. In fact the good Reverend had to go back to Padanaram. He had another church meeting to attend."

"Honey, you have a tick at the corner of your mouth. That's a sign of anger, isn't it?"

"Do I really?"

One of the deputies shivered and reached to turn up the thermostat.

"You're not mad at *me*, are you?"

"I think I have good reason to be. Not every woman shouts for joy when she gets left at the altar."

"All this even before you've heard my explanation?"

"Oh, no, I'm fully prepared to hear your explanation—if you have one." Rose whirled around, her skirts flying, as she searched for a chair. Pete obliged. "Thank you, Mr. Wilkins," she said as she settled in and gave Sam Horton a piercing glare. "Now then, Mr. Horton, please go ahead with your explanation, if any."

"Oh, brother," Sam groaned. "Bring the guilty rascal in and give him a fair trial before we hang him."

"An excellent idea," Rose said. "Please hurry. I don't think your daughter is too happy about all the delay, and your father said something about getting back to Boston before dark."

"Rats deserting the sinking ship," he snarled. "I never expected that of my father."

"Time's a'wasting, Mr. Horton."

Another deputy came into the room while Sam fumbled around for something to say. What he *really* wanted to say was something in the order of, To hell with it all, but that was hardly appropriate. Too much of his life was bound up in this little bundle of femininity and he was not about to cast it over the side. "Damn you," he muttered as he stepped forward and wrapped her up in his arms.

For just a moment there was resistance, a struggle to free herself from his grip. But then, without any real pressure, his lips came down on hers. Gently, warmly, the sort of kiss that she enjoyed. The kind of kiss that sent little tremors up from her stomach to her brain. The kind of kiss that brought her arms up around his neck and cuddled her cheek against his throat. When he ran out of breath he released her, but instead of moving away she pulled herself closer.

"Is the wedding off?" he murmured.

"Not a chance," she snapped. "I'm going to teach you a lesson, Mr. Horton. I'm going to marry you and teach you a very sharp lesson."

"God, that *will* be something," he said as he applied pressure again.

The deputy who had recently come into the room had brought a handcuffed prisoner with him. "They told me I should bring this guy up here," he announced. Rose and Sam slacked off their lines and turned to look.

"Chad Westbrook!" Rose hissed.

"Well, so it is," Sam said. "Want to start where we left off out at the post office?"

"Keep that man away from me!" Chad's teeth were chattering as he backed off into a corner, carrying the deputy with him.

"Sam Horton, what did you do to Westbrook over at the post office?" Rose asked.

Sam shrugged. "Nothing much," he said. "He made some remark about my girlfriend, so I gave him a double whammy—and he fell down, right in front of a police car. I told you once before that I have a lot of luck—all bad. Can you imagine that? Absolutely not an ounce of gentility in him. And you said he came from an old-line Yankee family. Hah! Fourth Generation, I suppose."

"Well, there's always one bad apple in every barrel," Rose said. "How come he's wearing handcuffs and you're not?"

"Because he's charged with larceny and attempted murder by automobile, and your husband is only charged with assault and battery," the officer behind Chad said. And then he said, to the other deputy, "The DA said we have to get our hands on this woman who lost all that money. Mrs. Chase—Mrs. Rose Chase. Probably another one of those rich little old ladies down in Padanaram. The village is loaded with 'em."

He turned back to Sam with a smile. "And that, Horton, was what you ought to have been doing: hunting around for a rich widow and marrying her. It would have been a lot better than working for the attorney general."

"Just a minute," Rose said. "Run that by me one more time."

"What? About Horton?"

"Yes, about Horton."

"Well, first of all when we picked him up on this assault charge he kept claiming that he was working undercover for the attorney general. Something about fraud cases down in Padanaram. There are lots of women down there who have inherited a slew of money, and one or two people have been putting the bite on them."

"I'm sure my fiancée doesn't care to hear any more about anything like that," Sam protested. "On the other hand, she's very fond of Penny Horton, and I'm sure she'd be interested in that hit-and-run case."

"I'm sure she wouldn't," Chad Westbrook chipped in. "A minor auto accident—"

"Sam Horton," Rose interrupted, frozen-faced. "Working for the attorney general? We're going to have a few words, you and I!"

"After the wedding," Sam pleaded.

"Funny thing," the deputy said. "Hit-and-run. We've got half a dozen on the books, and all of a sudden the Dartmouth police, the district attorney and the state police all received copies of a picture showing a garage out in Nonquit, in which the very car we've been looking for was parked. Westbrook's car."

"My goodness, what a coincidence," Rose said sweetly. "So you went out and arrested him?"

"Didn't have to, ma'am. He came in with Horton here, who was arrested for assault. Just the man we were looking for, Westbrook is. The state police had only just called us about this garage business when in he walked. So we grabbed him. We have to make some more tests, but the district attorney is sure we have the right monkey by the tail."

"Wonderful," Rose said, her face lighting up like a new moon. "And that's why you were late for the wedding, Sam? It had better be!"

"The very reason," he said hastily. "What time is it now?"

"Six-thirty," Rose said after consulting her watch.

"Still time for us to get back to the hospital and the wedding?"

"Only we've lost the minister who was going to conduct the service."

"Was this all planned for St. Luke's?" the deputy asked.

"Yes," Sam explained. "My daughter's hospitalized, and we planned to get married in the children's ward."

"Mice and men," the deputy said. "Too bad."

"But say, there's always some churchman on call for the hospital," the other deputy said. "You could call up there, they could call in the stand-by preacher, and we could ride you up to the hospital in a squad car."

"Even with the sirens?" Rose asked excitedly. The one thing she had always wanted was a ride in a police car with the siren going.

"With the siren going," the officer promised. "C'mon."

"But what about this other guy?"

"The DA will be here in a few minutes to grill him." The inner door swung open, and the district attorney came in as if on stage cue.

"What's going on?" Gomez said.

"Well, that's the Westbook guy," the officer said. "Hit-and-run, massive larceny. You wanted to talk to him."

"So I did. Did you find this Mrs. Chase?"

"Not yet. We were gonna run this pair up to the hospital so they can get married. It seems that while we were trying to confirm that Mr. Horton here worked for the attorney general we blew their three o'clock wedding."

"And my daughter's a patient," Sam said, "and also the flower girl."

"What a nice thing," Mr. Gomez said, remembering that he needed a good many votes in the next election, and the vote projection his campaign manager had just explained to him. "But—"

"But?" Rose and Sam exclaimed at the same time.

"But we can't just turn this guy loose. The judge set his bail at five hundred dollars. No pay, no go!"

"But he's a hero," Rose interjected.

"Shut up, Rose," Sam hissed at her quietly. "If they ever find out who took those pictures—"

Rose stumbled over a noun or two and then clamped her hand over her mouth.

"Then you can pay the bail?"

"Not a chance. I spent all my money on—family photos—you remember. Have you got five hundred dollars in your purse?"

Rose fumbled around and found less than two dollars. "Listen, Mr. District Attorney, we don't have that much, but I'm well-known in Padanaram. Perhaps you could—"

"Are you?" the DA said, chuckling. "You may be just the woman I've been looking for. Judge Pendergast is holding a hearing at ten tonight, and I need this Rose

Chase for a witness. I might have to lock her up until the hearing's over. Would you happen to know her?"

Rose, a faithful member of the Episcopal Church, looked them all straight in the eye and said, "I've never heard of her."

"Too bad," the DA said. "Well, your Mr. Horton could always get out tomorrow. Too bad. That's Doug Fishman going down the corridor. He's a bail bondsman."

"What the devil does a bail bondsman do?" Rose whispered, loudly enough for Mr. Fishman to hear.

"I help out," he said to Rose. "Somebody needs bail, I put it up, providing you people have some security to offer. I get a little interest off the top, of course."

"I need five hundred dollars," Rose gasped. "Right now."

"Cash on the barrel head," Fishman said. "What have you got for security?"

Shaking her head sadly, Rose unfastened the eighteen-thousand-dollar wristwatch that had been her mother's treasure. "Might this do?" she asked meekly.

The diamond-inset numbers sparkled in the dim light of the courthouse, outlined against the gold frame. "Holy—!" the bail bondsman said.

"Get the car," the DA ordered. "And watch the siren. We've had too many police accidents this month already."

"For eighteen thousand dollars I don't even get sirens?" Rose asked plaintively. But Sam was already leading her out of the building.

CHAPTER TEN

EIGHT o'clock in the evening, on the second Tuesday of September. Sam followed the police car as closely as possible. Rose had appropriated the front seat of the squad car, its red and blue lights flashing, its siren roaring at innocent bystanders. Until it came within a block of the hospital, where the driver shut it off, with an apology.

"No need to apologize," Rosie said, chortling. "I haven't had so much fun since I went to Disney World about twenty years ago."

"Yeah, well, then, we're all happy," the police driver said. "We caught that embezzler, and that hit-and-run driver. Gawd, you've got no idea what a pleasure it is to catch the guy who ran down that little girl. Got any kids of your own?"

"One," Rosie said. "My daughter, Penny, was the girl who was run down. Do you suppose he could get life in prison, plus ten years?"

"I doubt it, ma'am. I'd count on six to ten. But he's got another problem. There's nothing that convicts hate worse than a child-abuser. When they send him up to the pen and the inmates hear what he's in for, they'll work him over. That's doin' hard time, that is. Here you are. The elevators are just inside the double door. And lady—"

"Rosie," she said, just barely cutting off her last name.

"Rosie, have a good life, my dear."

"And the same to you and yours," Rose said as she climbed out of the car. In a moment the police car was gone and Sam's van had taken its place.

"Why, Rosie," he said softly. "Crying?"

169

"A nice man just said a nice thing to me," she explained. "And I don't have a handkerchief."

"Here. I always carry two." He whipped a massive handkerchief out of his coat pocket and passed it over to her. She used it to dry the tears as he took her arm and hurried her to the door. Is that true? she thought. You always carry two? Sam Horton, you are just on the border of superperfection. I must have a talk with your mother some time soon. Dare I say you're too good to be true?

"What did you say?" The elevator was standing in front of them, open and empty.

"Just clearing my throat, love," Rose Mary lied.

The elevator did its bit at top speed, and disgorged them at the lobby of the children's ward. Everything was quiet. All but the night lights were out.

"Lord love us," Rose whispered. "We're too late."

"Don't you believe it," Sam said. "I'm in charge now."

"Yes, sir," she replied.

"Now and for ever," he said. Rose mulled that over for a few seconds. It seemed to be a long-term sort of promise. He was a wonderful man, but, after all, he was only a man.

"I'll tell you what I'll do," she said. "If you can get us married tonight in Penny's presence, without us getting arrested again, I'll agree."

He grinned down at her, picked her up off her feet, and kissed her tenderly. "You don't think it's possible, do you, Rosie, gal?" He set her back on her tiny feet and grinned again.

"And don't call me Rosie," she murmured.

"Whatever you say, Rosie." He took her hand and towed her down the ward until they ran into the night nurse.

"Visiting hours are over," the nurse said.

"You're new on this ward, Nurse, aren't you?"

"Yes. This is my first night in the hospital."

"Has she gone?"

"Who?"

"My daughter, Penny. We were told that she couldn't last much longer, so we got a police escort to bring us in. We promised the child we would get married at her bedside before—before—"

"Oh, the poor child. I haven't had a chance to check all the charts, and nothing about this was included in the day briefing reports. I—what would you like me to do?"

"Don't cry, Rose." This was said with unctuous cheer, accompanied by a sharp nudge in her ribs from his elbow. Rose took the cue, and turned on the water-works.

"Nurse, could you page the hospital chaplain? It wouldn't take much time. If he could come up right away and marry us, then Penny could be happy."

The three of them had moved slowly down the aisle, and at this last moment they were standing by the foot of Penny's bed.

"What are you guys makin' all this noise for?" the girl whispered.

"That's Penny, Nurse. Hit by a car, you know. Hit-and-run."

"I'll get the chaplain paged," the nurse said. "Poor, poor child. Lord, I need a handkerchief."

"Dad, what kind of a scam are you working to-night?" Penny said. "I was almost asleep, and—"

"You can sleep tomorrow," her father said. "Right now we're getting married, and you—"

"Why is Mama cryin'?"

"Because you're in the hospital," Sam said. "We have to perform this little act. It's a short ceremony, but you're dying, so you have to groan a time or two here and there."

"I'm dying?"

"No, you're *not* dying. You don't even have a headache. But the nurse, *she* thinks you're dying, so if you want us to get married tonight you have to *act* like you're dying. Got it?"

"Sam Horton," Rose interjected, "what in the world am I marrying? First you're a cruel-hearted lawyer, then you're a burglar, then you assault and batter Chad, and now you're turning our daughter into a—"

"And now he's the nicest father a girl ever had," Penny interrupted. "Although I must admit you hafta be fast on your toes to keep up. Don't worry, Mama, I'll help you."

"Well, thank the Lord for little favors," Rose said as she dropped into the chair by Penny's bed. A pair of rascals, she told herself. But given a little time I'll get them both straightened out. After all, what's a nice girl like me doing in the crowd like this? I will get them straightened out. But just at that moment she looked sidewise at the pair of them and noted the grins they were sharing. "Won't I?" she murmured to the Lord above.

"What?" Sam asked.

"Nothing," Rose said, and settled back into the chair.

"Then look, Rosie."

"Don't call her Rosie," his daughter said.

"After tomorrow," he said firmly, "I'll call her whatever I damn well please. Furthermore, I could do with considerably fewer instructions and commands from women! Got it?"

"Don't count me among your female slaves," Penny insisted. "I'm independent. Completely so. And if I get any more lip I'm gonna go and live with Millie."

"Here comes the Reverend," Sam said, hushing them. "I'm gonna speed out into the hall and give him a briefing. Remember, daughter—groan a little."

"Yeah. Groan a little," Penny said. "Rose?"

"Not me, love. I see myself fixed for life. I'm going to marry Sam, and he's going to support me for the rest of my life. And your father is going to feed and clothe and house me, till death us do part! And maybe a little longer than that."

"Wow, have you got it made," Penny said. "I never realized what an easy life it could be."

"Not to worry," Rose said. "I'll teach you how to do it. It's not too difficult."

"Just a darn minute," Sam said. "Oh, good evening, Reverend. This is my prospective bride, and my daughter, Penelope."

The priest was a painfully thin young black man, dressed typically in a black suit and a white Roman collar. For the first time Rose felt guilty—about almost everything in the world.

"I—Father," she stammered. "I'm not a Roman Catholic."

The priest looked down at Penny, who also might have been struck by an attack of conscience. "Me neither," the girl said, turning those dramatically beautiful eyes on him.

The priest looked over at Sam, who was about his size but obviously almost eighty pounds heavier. Sam shrugged and offered a weak grin. "So you've caught us," he said. "Neither am I."

The priest smiled beatifically at all of them as he set his little case on the bed and pulled out a stole and a cap. "Well, that makes it even," he said. "I'm Father Flannigan from St. Eugenie African Methodist Episcopal Church."

He whispered the service. Once the little boy in the adjoining bed awoke and whimpered. The night nurse comforted the child, and moments later the service continued.

"Love, honor and cherish," Father Flannigan said. It startled Rose. She had been floating, dreamlike, above the group. And she had truly expected him to say "Love, honor and obey". And Lord knew what she might have answered, but Sam nudged her gently—well, perhaps not all that gently.

"I do," she said, and for a second tried to back away. That was the turning point, Sam had said a half-dozen times. Right after "I do", and he was the boss for ever and ever. But Sam had a grip on her elbow. She looked up at him, and there was that wolfish grin, that grin of anticipation on his face. Remembering all the things he had said in the past weeks, Rose felt her feet beginning to run. The priest said something about "for ever and ever. Amen". And the service was over.

There was a deep silence. "You may kiss the bride," the night nurse said. The young priest blushed, nodded, and repacked his little case. Sam, who obviously didn't know where the nurse's part was written in the service, was willing to cooperate. He lifted Rose an inch or two above the floor, and kissed her gently before setting her down again.

"There," he said. "It's done."

But Rose was disappointed. She'd thought it would be a little more passionate. Some burning, triumphant kiss that might have burned the words into their minds. Instead, it had been like kissing Millie!

So she leaned over and kissed Penny, who did much better. Not passionate, of course, but certainly loving. "Good idea," Sam whispered, and leaned over to kiss the princess in his turn. But unfortunately she had already fallen asleep, worn out by all the ceremony, and reacting to the shot she had received to prepare her for the morning's operation.

They signed a few papers. The priest, the nurse, her assistant, Sam, and, finally, Rose Mary Horton. It was a nice feeling all round. Then they tiptoed out of the

ward, and Sam made some sort of contribution to Father
Flannigan. Rose couldn't see what the contribution was,
but it was green, and the priest thrust it into his pocket
and almost choked.

"And now," Sam said, "let's go home, shall we?"

And this, Rose Horton told herself, is where I ought
to start running.

Sam took her arm and ushered her into the elevator.
Rose, who knew all about the birds and the bees, having
been married once before, albeit for a short time, still
shivered. There was no way that Sam Horton could be
compared to dear Frank. Not in size, knowledge, determination or dominance. And so she shivered again.

"Cold, Rosie?"

"I—perhaps a little."

"There's a blanket on the back seat of the van." He
opened the door for her and pushed her up the step. She
snatched at the blanket, threw it around her hurriedly,
and huddled in a corner of the second seat.

Sam climbed into the van behind her and slammed
the door shut.

"You can't drive from back here," Rose said.

"No? Perhaps not. But then I thought I would take
a minute or two and accomplish some business before
we drive off."

"Here? In the back of the van?"

"Here, Rosie, gal."

"Don't call me—" But she remembered his warnings,
and shut down on her conversation. If that's the way he
wants it, she told herself, who am I to quibble? And
when he sat down close beside her, and one of his hands
came around her shoulders, she took a deep breath, said
a short prayer, and hoped.

His free hand loosened the blanket. For a moment she
felt a cold wind blowing in on her. But when he pulled
her closer the warmth returned. He picked up the end
of the blanket and managed to make it into a shelter.

The warmth increased. One hand crept across from her shoulder and gently touched the curve of her breast. She drew a sharp breath. Don't jump, she told herself. We're married. He has rights.

His hand explored further, undoing her zipper and then slipping inside, seeking her soft breasts. I should have worn a bra, she told herself, but it was too late. And besides, she liked what was happening. A soft touch brought her nipple to attention. Rose Horton gasped at the flashing sensations that followed. Frank had never done anything like that. She relaxed, and let the joy flow—

Until somebody outside banged on the side of the van. "What the hell ... ?" Sam muttered as he struggled up to peer out the window. "Oh, no!"

"You can't park here for billing and cooing," the hospital security officer said. He banged the side of the van one more time with his baton, to make his point.

"Okay," Sam called. "Okay. We were just leaving."

"Sure you were," the officer said sarcastically. "Try starting the motor. It helps when you want to get a van this size moving."

"Wise guy," Sam muttered as he moved up to the driver's seat and stuck the key into the ignition. The motor roared. Rose, still embarrassed, zipped her dress back up—no easy task—and wished that nothing like this had ever happened. In fact, it never had before. Frank had been unable to play games in automobiles, and Rose had always maintained a cool front with boys, just as her mother had always lectured.

"Don't worry," Sam told her as he zoomed out of the parking lot and onto Page Street. "We'll be home in a minute."

"I'm sure we will," Rose said hesitantly. The tears were silent; she desperately tried to stem them. Not that she was afraid, pained, concerned. It was just because she felt—frustrated by it all.

They were home on Middle Street by midnight. Millie heard the van drive up and had the front door open when they came up the walk. "Ah, poor Rose," she said, embracing her. "I've heard some of the story. Your mother called me, Sam. All that trouble and you couldn't get married!"

"Oh, we got married all right," Rose said. "But you wouldn't believe what a problem it was. We were married by the Reverend Hannigan—"

"Flannigan," Sam interjected.

"Yeah. Flannigan. Of the African Methodist Episcopal Church." Rose sighed and headed for the kitchen. "Millie, I'm dying for a cup of coffee."

And the call for midnight coffee was immediately followed by the offer of a full meal. Their animals clung to them, never wanting to give up. Even Beatrice, the elderly cat, horned in on the act.

"I don't know where they'll sleep," Millie cautioned. "The kittens are pretty well trained to the cat box. Beatrice and Rudolph sleep where they please. More steak, Sam?"

"No, thanks, Millie. I swear I have had enough. All good, of course, as usual, but enough."

"You wouldn't say anything if it wasn't," Millie retorted. "Typical man. Well, I don't intend to sit up all night and choke food down your faces."

"Good Lord," Rose said. "Look at that clock. It's three in the morning. Can that be the right time?"

"That clock hasn't been wrong since World War II," Millie said.

"Well, that settles it," Rose decreed. "Us for bed, Mr. Horton."

"Right behind you, Mrs. Horton. But please remember that you said 'I do' tonight, and from now on I'll give the orders in this family."

"I can't fight that," Rosie said. "Are you going to carry me upstairs?"

"You've got that a little mixed up," he said. "That's carry you over the threshold—not up two flights of stairs."

"So there *is* something you can't do," Rose teased.

"There are lots of things I can't do," he said. "I can, for example, easily carry you up the stairs. Unfortunately, once we got up there I wouldn't be worth a wooden nickel, and you wouldn't like that!"

"You'd better believe that's true," she told him as she took his hand—or he took her hand—and they chased each other up the stairs.

"What do you know?" mused Millie. The two kittens were asleep in their little cardboard box. Beatrice was camped out under the stove in the kitchen. But Rudolph, still not fully recovered, although he was being fed well, and often, was too restless. He had been napping under Millie's kitchen rocking chair. Now, at the departure of the newlyweds, he grumbled, stretched, and made his way slowly up the stairs. Beatrice, the old cat, opened one eye, saw his departure, and trailed along behind.

It had been months since Rose had slept in the master bedroom. Now, in the pale moonlight, she pirouetted in the middle of the room and took a deep breath. Laid out on top of the emperor-sized bed was a diaphanous white silk nightgown.

"You get first shower," her lord and master said. "But don't dilly."

Rose snatched up the nightgown. Rolled up in her hand, it made something a little smaller than a softball. She giggled as she went by him. He reached out and patted her on her well-rounded flank. She managed another laugh, but the pat was not all that soft. In fact, once inside the bathroom she rubbed the spot and climbed under the hot water, hoping to relieve the sting.

"Don't dilly", he had said. And she wouldn't. She was out in a matter of minutes.

The bathroom was well steamed. It was difficult to dry herself off in the face of the humidity. But she struggled. There was no sense in washing her hair. She had something more important to do. The nightgown was a little loose. She clambered into it, brushed her hair, and opened the door into the bedroom. The room was empty.

"Lord," she asked the empty room, "isn't anything going to go right for me?" The French door that led out onto the little upper balcony came open and Sam, stripped to his trousers, came back in.

"Ooph!" Rose commented as she dived for the bed. She knew a little bit about men, did Rosie Horton. They liked to find their new bride already in the bed, waiting. She managed to straighten out her fall of hair so that he wouldn't land on it and tear a few chunks out in the doing. Her mother had told her about that. And then she lay back and listened to the shower with anticipation.

The bedside clock said three-thirty, and Sam came out, clothed in a towel wrapped around his neck. The bathroom light, still on, outlined him in all his detail. Rose gasped. There was—so much of him. Men come in different sizes, she reminded herself. But how does one handle a full-sized male? Handle? Luckily he had flipped the bathroom light off. Lucky for me, Rose told herself as the bed sagged.

"You need more room?" she asked hesitantly.

"Stay right where you are," he responded. "I think we can make some arrangement." He moved a little closer. His left arm slipped under her neck and around her shoulders and pulled her closer. She nestled up against him, savoring her good luck. His other hand came across her bosom, touching for a moment where her nightgown did not cover. Quickly his hand slid under her gown, touched down on her breast, and treasured it. Rose shivered. I've done a lot of that lately, she told herself, but it was so pleasant that—that she nestled closer up against the hard wall of his chest.

And at that moment something went bump-bump-bump at the door, accompanied by a scratching sound. More bumps. "What the hell?" Sam said as the door slid open and banged against the stops.

Rudolph made a polite bark of announcement and paraded into the room. He walked up to the bed. Beatrice, beside him, leaped up onto the coverlet, dug herself a circle among the blankets, and settled down. Rudolph, not to be outdone, managed to vault clumsily up between them, beating Rose's knees with his tail and resting his heavy muzzle on Sam's shoulder.

"Go away," Sam ordered. The two animals paid not the slightest bit of attention.

"Oh, Gawd," Rosie said. "Do something. You're the man of the house."

"Rose," he said, sighing, "sometimes you talk too much!"

In the middle of her internal debate, while Sam was giving serious thought to taking some action, Rose fell fast asleep—leaving her new husband more frustrated than ever!

"Five o'clock," Millie said as she shook the pair of them. "Penny goes into the operating room at six. You'll want to see her before she goes down. Right?"

"Yeah, right," Penny's father groaned as he rolled over and went back to sleep.

"Rose? Shake a leg, Rose. Time to go back to the hospital."

"Call Sam," Rose grumbled. "He's the kid's father."

"I did. He just went back to sleep."

"I'll get him," Rose promised. "If I can't sleep, why should he?"

Some minutes later the pair of them stumbled down the stairs, preceded by their animal friends. The two kittens, excited by the new world of things, raced around the kitchen, jumping up toward available laps, doing their best to share breakfasts.

"Now that's enough of that," Millie said. "I don't make eggs and sausages for kittens. You hear me?" They acted as if they did, but made no effort to correct their behavior. "Shoo," Millie yelled at them.

Rose did her best to eat with delicacy, as befitting an old married woman. Sam made no such attempt. He wielded knife and fork as if he were a Norse adventurer. As a result, by the time he completed his meal Rose was only halfway through, and being coaxed to hurry. Which she did, thinking of the poor little girl in that darkened hospital ward up in the city.

"You drive," Sam said.

"Me? I haven't driven in ages. No, thank you."

"Spoilsport."

So he guided them through the dark, almost empty streets. Rose had intended to pray. She ended up napping. They arrived at the hospital parking lot at about five forty-five, only to find that Penny had already been taken downstairs.

Finding where "downstairs" was took more effort than they knew. It was not until they ran into a sleepy intern on his way to the same destination that they had any sort of luck. There were a couple of lounges for waiting surgery patients on the first floor. Next to the lounges was a large waiting room where the patients were assembled, two or three at a time, and given their preparatory shots. Penny was waiting sleepily on a gurney, her eyes half-swollen with sleep, an intravenous tube inserted in her arm, and a red spot where she had already been administered a shot.

"I thought you guys wasn't comin'," she sputtered, and held out her hands for hugs and kisses. "Mama?"

"Right here," Rose said, bending over to kiss her. "Don't you look pretty. They've painted your left leg in all the colors of the rainbow. Why would they do that?"

"I dunno," Penny said. "Believe me, they never tell me nothin'."

"Me neither," said the burly surgeon in greens who came over behind them, masked. "Penelope Horton, huh?"

He was doing something with the tube inserted in her arm. "You ain't gonna put that big needle in me, are you?" Penny begged.

"Not in you, sweetheart. It goes right here in this tube, and the tube doesn't feel a thing, now does it?"

"It didn't say anything," the wit of the Horton family said. "Now what?"

"Can you count to one hundred?"

"Sure."

"Then you do that," the surgeon instructed. Penny started off at half-speed, made it up to ten, slowed perceptibly at fifteen, and by the time she reached nineteen she was burbling away, out like a light.

"Now we'll take her along to one of the operating rooms," the surgeon said. "We'll start the operation in about a half-hour, and probably finish it around two hours after that. You can meet her again right here in the recovery room at about that time. Right?"

"And what are her chances?" a nervous Sam Horton asked.

"Chances? Eighty-five percent for a complete success. Two percent for a failure."

Three hours later, back in the same room, Penny Horton stirred, looked around and said, "When are they gonna start, Mama?"

Sam, who realized that he had lost his daughter to his new wife, grinned down at her. "Well, to tell the truth, love," he said, "it's all over."

"Well, I'll be darned," the child said as she closed her eyes and went back to sleep.

There was nothing more for the elder Hortons to do. They walked out in the sunshine for a bit, met with Sam's father and mother, and talked about how it was when *they* were young. When Penny awakened all four of them visited again, and then they were thrust out in the cold by the various nurses.

"Tyrants," Rose commented as they made their way out to the truck. "Now what do we do, Sam?"

"I'm given to understand that there are a couple of policemen waiting to talk to us," he replied. "And *then* we'll go home—"

"And take a nap?" Rose said wistfully.

"And take a nap," he agreed. Rose watched his sparkling brown eyes. There was no doubt what sort of a nap he was thinking about. A little shiver ran up and down her spine. She was thinking of exactly the same thing!

The two policemen were standing by their Dartmouth squad car, enjoying as much of the sun as they could find.

"Mrs.—er—Horton?"

"Yes?"

"We've had a couple of unusual things happen, Mrs. Horton. You might perhaps remember that we received a hot tip a few hours ago, and we found the car that was involved in a hit-and-run accident with your—stepdaughter."

"I remember," Rose said. "And—"

"And the man who evidently drove that car was also the man who embezzled some money from you?"

"Oh, that part you have to take up with my husband," Rose said. "He's also my lawyer."

"In that case, Mr. Horton, the district attorney would like to consult with you about this man."

"I can do that," Sam said, sighing. "Right after I get some sleep, please."

"Just as soon as you can," the officer said. "At least before noontime. Because we've found another case to press against him."

"Oh?"

"Well, you might not remember that this same man was involved in another hit-and-run accident a year ago, in which he killed a crippled guy. Frank Hamilton was the victim's name."

"Dear God," Rose cried in pained disbelief. "My first husband, Frank was."

"It's hard to believe, ma'am. Two hit-and-run cases within three blocks of each other. We suspect the man was drunk, but we never did catch up to him to prove it—until now. His second car was an Italian Ferrari, and he had it buried in a sand pile out behind his barn."

"Oh, Lord, look what you've done." Sam Horton sighed. Rose Mary felt a blur as the sun became too much for her. She crumpled slowly to the ground like a piece of waste paper, and had it not been for Sam's quick reaction she would have fallen into the flowerbeds.

"Millie, I don't know what to say. I had to leave her at the hospital. I don't know what's the matter. These damn medical people have a language you wouldn't believe. She's suffering from—"

"Shock trauma," Millie interrupted.

"Damn," the frustrated lawyer said. "And I've got to go see the district attorney in—my lord, twenty minutes. Where in the world are Rose's papers?"

"There's a big box in the closet of the living room. Or, if you're talking about money and stuff, she had everything on four of those five-inch disks, and they're all stuffed in the back of her computer."

"I'll take everything," Sam said. "Where the devil did I put my marriage certificate—and that power of attorney?"

"How would I know?" Millie said softly as he banged his way out the door. "Men!"

So, what with one thing and another, it was Friday before Sam Horton was reunited with his bride. "I've already checked on Penny," he said. "She's doing well. In fact they say she can come home by next Wednesday. Climb in. We're going home."

"I like that," Rose said. "Could you—?"

"Hurry? I'm hurrying! Or do I interpret you wrongly?"

She grinned up at him. "Hurry," she said.

He did, of course. Until they were almost at the foot of Dartmouth Street. "I have to hurry," he explained to the policeman in the patrol car.

"Yes, I did notice," the cop said as he whipped out his ticket book.

"But this is our honeymoon trip," Rose complained plaintively.

"Well, now, congratulations. That will be a seventy-five-dollar fine. You can either mail it in to the district court or you can appeal for a hearing in front of a judge."

Sam's color rose. "Look, you don't seem to—"

"We'll mail it in," Rose assured the cop. "Thank you ever so much."

And off they went, over to Middle Street. Millie was out somewhere, but the animals welcomed them with noisy approval.

"Upstairs, Rose Mary Horton," he ordered.

"Ah. This is where we get that bit about you chief, me squaw?"

"Upstairs. I've got an errand to do."

So, being an obedient and loving wife, Rose scooted upstairs. Something was going on downstairs. The dog was yelping, Beatrice the cat was yowling, and the two kittens were evidently kicking up a fuss. Rose shrugged, peeled herself out of her blue suit, and, totally naked, bounced herself off the middle of the bed and giggled.

In less than five minutes Sam came running up the stairs. His shirt was off, his shoes bounced on the hall landing, and he was unzipping his trousers as he came.

"Had to leave them all some food," he reported, gasping. "And tied them up."

"Good show," she said. "Now—"

"I know." He rolled over on top of her. "Now, where was I?" One of his hands stroked her breast. Rose moaned and wrapped her legs around him. He teased her until she could hardly wait another minute.

"C'mon," she said. "I can't—"

And the telephone rang.

"Let it ring," he said, but the interruption had spoiled the whole routine.

"It might be something about Penny," his wife gasped.

Sam reached over and picked up the telephone. His ardor was gone. "Hello," he answered.

"Hello, Mr. Horton."

"Yes? What is it?"

"I'm calling from Sears and Roebuck, Mr. Horton. We want you to know that we have a photo special for you and your brand-new wife, and—"

"Sears and Roebuck?" he roared. "Listen, lady. I'll kill them both. And you too. And your husband. And all six of your kids, if you have any. You hear me?"

"May I take that as a rejection?" the operator asked.

"You certainly damn well can," Sam roared as he threw the telephone underneath the bed and fell back, flat on his back.

"That's funny," Rose Horton said, giggling.

"The hell you say," Sam Horton said.

And they both broke out laughing.

EPILOGUE

SPRINGTIME came early in the following year. The birds were out, gleefully bombing the assembled fleet in Padanaram harbor, and as soon as the snow was melted Penny Horton was at the front door.

"Walk, Mother?" she yelled up the stairs.

Millie came out of the kitchen, a big smile on her face. Rose came slowly down the stairs. "What did your father say?" she asked suspiciously.

"Walk," the girl said. "And the doctor said the same. Walk, just as soon as the ice is gone. And what did *your* doctor say, Mrs. Horton?"

"Walk," Rose admitted. "And don't be a smart kid. But I wish your father was here. You need a jacket."

"And so do you, Ma." But Millie was already there, holding coats for each of them. And the front door opened.

"All my girls are going for a walk?" Sam Horton asked as he came in. "The way the doctor prescribed? For both of you?"

"If I had known what a witty fellow your father was," Rose told Penny, "I might have reconsidered this marriage business."

"Don't tell me," Penny retorted, "tell him. As far as I can see you're only half-right!"

"And you," Rose snapped at Sam, "cut out the smirk. I wouldn't be in all this trouble if it wasn't for you!"

"C'mon," Penny insisted as she opened the door. "I wanna show you something." And she skipped out into the yard, did a little dance to demonstrate her new-found agility, and came back to them, grinning. She tried to

188

hug her mother, but just couldn't reach all the way around.

"Well, I can't dance," Rose said, sighing. "Not for another two months."

"I don't know about havin' another girl around the house," Penny said thoughtfully.

"Then you have nothing to worry about," Rose Mary chuckled. "My doctor and I had this little exercise with the magic-machine this morning. It's going to be a boy."

"Oh, great," Penny said half-heartedly.

"Hey, great," Sam Horton said with a great deal of enthusiasm. "A boy-child!"

"Yes," Rose said cheerfully. "A boy-child. Aren't I clever? I thought I might name him after an old friend of mine. Chadwick. An old New England name."

"If you do you'll sleep alone," Sam threatened. "Come over here. I can still hug you both at the same time."

"Sleeping alone wouldn't be all that much fun," Rose admitted as she squeezed in between the pair of them. "Maybe I could name him Steven. After your grandfather, love. Come on, you two, let's walk!"

And hard-hearted Millie, standing at the front window listening and watching, snatched up her apron and wiped a happiness-tear from the corner of her eye before she shooed the three cats and the dog back into the kitchen where the cookies were baking.

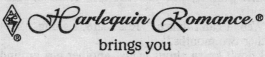

BRIDE'S BAY RESORT

UNLOCK THE DOOR TO GREAT ROMANCE AT BRIDE'S BAY RESORT

Join Harlequin's new across-the-lines series, set in an exclusive hotel on an island off the coast of South Carolina.

Seven of your favorite authors will bring you exciting stories about fascinating heroes and heroines discovering love at Bride's Bay Resort.

Look for these fabulous stories coming to a store near you beginning in January 1996.

Harlequin American Romance #613 in January
Matchmaking Baby by Cathy Gillen Thacker

Harlequin Presents #1794 in February
Indiscretions by Robyn Donald

Harlequin Intrigue #362 in March
Love and Lies by Dawn Stewardson

Harlequin Romance #3404 in April
Make Believe Engagement by Day Leclaire

Harlequin Temptation #588 in May
Stranger in the Night by Roseanne Williams

Harlequin Superromance #695 in June
Married to a Stranger by Connie Bennett

Harlequin Historicals #324 in July
Dulcie's Gift by Ruth Langan

Visit Bride's Bay Resort each month wherever Harlequin books are sold.

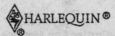

HARLEQUIN ®

BBAYG

HARLEQUIN PRESENTS®

Harlequin brings you the best books, by the best authors!

MIRANDA LEE

"...another scandalously sensual winner"
—*Romantic Times*

&

LYNNE GRAHAM

"(Her) strong-willed, hard-loving characters are the sensual
stuff dreams are made of"—*Romantic Times*

Look out next month for:

MISTRESS OF DECEPTION by Miranda Lee
Harlequin Presents #1791

CRIME OF PASSION by Lynne Graham
Harlequin Presents #1792

Harlequin Presents—the best has just gotten better!
Available in February wherever Harlequin books are sold.

TAUTH-5